Lenah's Veil

A Midwife's Memoir

Chapter One

Sundays was my favorite days 'cause they was the only days we got to enjoy two good meals and plenty of rest and play.
Most mornings us would eat porridge or boiled corn meal with molasses. When Massa was in a good way, he'd give us extra rations.
This Sunday the womens in the quarter fried up pork skins, boiled potatoes and ho'cakes for breakfast.
I love me some ho'cakes with molasses.

Mama made sure me & Alice ate our share of the morning's rations~ while she got herself ready for the day. She spent the entire morning brushing her hair. I'll never forget that brush; it was brass with soft bristles all through it. Mama treasured that brush; she said her old Massa gave it to her.

Mama was the best looking colored woman I'd ever seen. She had golden brown skin, deep piercing almond-shaped eyes and beautiful full lips. She was tall and slender, with wavy brown hair that flowed down her back. I never understood why Mama spent all that time on her hair, only to cover it all up with that white head scarf of hers.

1

Boy, me and Alice cut up something terrible when she got to yanking that comb through our heads. She'd tell us our hair was just like hers, 'cept our curls was a little tighter. She ain't like it when we looked down on ourselves.

"I ain't have no ugly duckings", she'd tell us.

On Sundays all slaves was expected to worship at the Peyton family chapel right there on the plantation; but for us the real praising ain't start til nightfall.

We ain't worship God the same way we done at Peyton chapel neither. We sang louder, and danced like our very souls depended on it. In some way it did, since heaven was the only paradise us had to look forward to, at least that's how we seen it. Once us get to shouting, there wasn't no stopping.

Massa Peyton used to say us ought to be 'thankful' for what the good Lord gives us. Cato, one of the field hands always made us laugh mocking Massa Peyton,

"Be thankful Niggas for what ya'll gots now!" and in the same breath, he'd say,

"What us got to be thankful for?"

Lord that Cato could make a dead man laugh if he wanted. Maybe joking was his way of covering up all that pain he was feeling. I can't begins to tell you how awful them days was for our people.

Like I say, Cato had a way of taking our minds off our troubles. He had an eye for my Mama, too; he'd walk up on her nearly every day saying,

2

"Rachel, I'd throw whale oil over myself and run through hellfire for jest one kiss."

Mama wasn't bothered 'bout no Cato, all she cared 'bout was me, Alice, & Grandma Josie. She got attention like that all the time from mens in the quarter but they ain't dare fool 'round without Massa's approval. All us slaves belonged to Jesse Peyton; so wasn't nothing going down on that farm without his say so.

My friend Daisy lived in the shack two doors away from me with an old fieldhand called Silas. She asked me 'bout my pappy once – It wasn't no big deal I suppose ~ since she ain't know who her Mama or Pappy was. I jest told her the truth, I ain't know nothing 'bout him. Later, I thought about that question real hard. Mama never spoke 'bout my pap and I ain't think to question her back in them days. It ain't matter none anyhow; so I thought.

Massa used to tell us, that Nigras only good for breeding and entertainin'; nothing else – and for a long time I believed him. I reckon that's how him and his overseers kept us in line for so long. They'd say we no different than the horses and cattle he raised on that farm of his.

Horses and Cattle...can you imagine that?

Then I thought, when's the last time you heard a man ask a mule a question, and the mule answered him back?

Massa Peyton used to walk his way right up into our shack all hours of the night looking for my Mama. He ain't never bother to knock first; I s'pose he ain't need to.

Sometimes he'd bring mens in with him and other times he'd come by his'self. Mama used to beg Massa to make us

3

leave; most times he'd send us outside to wait until they finished with their business.

Alice and me used to wonder what they wanted with our Mama – when you a girl chile, you don't understand that sort of thing.

Sometimes Alice and me would wake up and find Mama gone the next morning – I reckon when they'd leave; she'd leave right out behind them. When she finally returned, she could barely look us in our faces.

We ain't dare question Mama on her whereabouts. Grandma Josie taught us to always respect Mama, no matter what. Besides, wasn't much Alice and me could do 'bout Mama's situation. Nobody dared sass Massa Peyton, for fear of what he was capable of doing to us. That man knew his way 'round a whip, and had no problem using it on us neither.

Me and Alice spent most days in them fields picking wheat, corn or whatever was in season. In between working, Massa would send for us to run around with his spoiled chillun', Hope and Carter.

Boy I tell you, us enjoyed having free time to play. A slave chile done just about anything to keep from working in them fields, and we wasn't no different.

I'll never forget Hope and Carter. When they got bored playing with one group of slave chillun', Massa would call on another bunch –I'll tell you, that man spoiled them 'chaps' rotten.

Each time we played against them Alice would say,

4

"Millie, don't give them their way, makes them earn their win."

We won at nearly every game us played against them, too. Alice was right, 'cause the more we won, the more they wanted to play with us. After a while they even started calling us their friends. Imagine that.

Mama and Grandma Josephine worried about us getting too comfortable with the Peyton kids. They'd tell us that nigra girls better off working out in them hot fields than running around all day trying to steer clear of Jesse Peyton.

Hmm! I used to think they was plum crazy saying that.

Massa was different with his own chillun'. He seemed like a real descent Pap; but us knew better. That man would act a 'down-right' fool when he'd show up around the slave quarter.

I used to ask myself, "At what point between the big house and the slave quarter did the devil jump into him?"

Alice and me was born on Peyton farm and besides field work, we spent our days doing other odd jobs around the place like cleaning, cooking and caring for slave chillun' in the quarter.

Mama told us that one day, when we came of age, that things was going to change. As much as she loved us, even more than her own life; she reminded us that we ain't belong to her. It ain't matter one bit that she gave birth to us; we was Jesse Peyton's property.

Sure enough, the morning after Alice's twelfth birthday, Massa Peyton came forcing his way up into the shack. He pulled Alice from our bed; still in her nightgown. He ain't say nothing at all, just started grabbing hold to her.

Mama took hold of Alice's leg, trying to keep Massa from getting her outside that shack. I remember Alice falling down at one point. There they were, Massa grabbing her by the arms and Mama pulling her by the legs.

I just stood there in shock; my body numb all over. There wasn't nothing I could do to help my poor sister and she knew it. Then Alice looked back at me with tears rolling down her face. Our eyes locked for a brief moment – and a strange feeling came over me. I couldn't explain it then, and I reckon I won't be able to explain it now. But I can tell you this much, I ain't never felt that desperate and helpless before in my entire life.

Massa was way too strong for Mama. He finally overcame Mama and pushed my sister outside. By that time a few overseers had arrived. I remember Alice standing in place gathering her bearings. Grandma Josephine rushed over after hearing the ruckus from a neighboring shack. Grandma tried to comfort Mama while at the same time begging Massa to leave Alice behind and take her instead.

That good-for-nothing wretch just laughed at them. Alice ain't speak one word, she knew wasn't no amount of reasoning going to sway that hard head of Jesse Peyton's. She held her head up high and boarded the wagon; she turned back one last time and placed her right hand over her heart. I reckon that was her way of telling us that she'd always love us.

Alice stayed calm, knowing full well that any other reaction would set Mama off again. She knew if she kept showing out than Massa Peyton would split the rest of us apart too. I was grateful for one thing that day; that the Lord gave my sister enough courage to stay calm the way she done that morning.

Mama wasn't the same after Massa took Alice away. She'd go out to them fields and barely lift a finger. When Massa got wind of it, he warned her that if she ain't start picking up her workload, he was going to sell her too!

That was the first time I remember hearing the word, 'Sell'.

Up to that day I ain't never pay much attention 'bout who came or went from the quarter; but after what happened to Alice, it was as though a bolt of lightening hit me. It was at that point I started paying real close attention to what was happening around there. Some folk call it "instinct". Whatever it was, I knew we wouldn't survive Peyton farm 'less we kept our wits about us.

During supper, when the men would gather 'round the bonfire, I'd keep my ears wide open listening to who did what, when and why they done it. I made it my business to know everybody else's business. You could say I grew up real fast on Peyton farm.

Then out of nowhere my luck started to change for the better. Massa got me away from them fields and put me in the kitchen on account of my relationship with Hope. Mama ain't like that one bit, she just knew Massa was up to no good and believed in her heart that he had it out for her.

I told Mama that I'd rather deal with Massa in the big house than labor all day in them hot fields alongside them no-count overseers of his.

Besides, I rather enjoyed helping the cooks and working 'round the big house. I got to wear fresh clothes everyday; not only that, working in the big house gave me a chance to get in good with the Peytons.

Miss Octavia was the mistress of the house. Everybody knew Massa had a wife but Miss Octavia never ever came 'round the slave quarter - Never. I reckon she wasn't trying to soil those fancy dresses of hers. She left the dirty work on the farm up to Massa Jesse. I always made a point of smiling politely in her presence; even complimented her every chance I got.

I figured if the Peytons ain't have no trouble using me, then I ain't have no reason not to use them right back.

Before too long though Mistress Peyton started taking somewhat of a liken to me. She eventually moved me from the shack I shared with Mama and grandma, into the servant's quarter next to the big house.

Mama ain't never say one bad word 'bout Miss Octavia moving me out; and I was real happy 'bout that too 'cause the servant's quarter was much better than that one-room shack I grew up in.

It wasn't too long before I started feeling real guilty 'bout leaving Mama & grandma. All I could think about was those nights when Mama and grandma's bellies was barely half- full, while I's sat back everyday eating high off of Massa's leftovers.

I used to believe that if I was patient enough and done whatever Miss Octavia asked, then maybe she'd have pity on us and talk that good- for-nothing husband of hers into giving' us our freedom.

Lord knows I wasn't holding my breath too long for that to happen.

One day, us prepared a nice lunch for the mistress and her friend, Mrs. Beverly. The mistress loved her visits with Mrs. Beverly – they was best friends. Them two talked about everything; even other mens.

Come to find out, Mistress and Massa Peyton was first cousins! I heard her tell Mrs. Beverly that Massa Peyton was the worse man she'd ever taken to bed with her. Then I overheard Mistress tell Mrs. Beverly 'bout her affair' with Isaac Burke; the son of Mayor Fenton Burke.

Mistress said Isaac knew a whole lot about pleasing a grown up woman, to be twenty-six years old. Miss Octavia and Mr. Isaac was carrying on relations like that the entire time she & Massa Peyton been married. Like I said, them womens were thick as thieves. Us knew they was up to no-good when them two got to cackling out loud, like two hens in a chicken coop.

Issac put a scare into Miss Octavia after he threatened to come-clean to Massa 'bout their affair. Somehow she convinced her young lover that he had a lot more to lose than she did, if he spilled the beans.
I declare, Miss Octavia was a 'mess'. She had mens swarming over her like bees on honey. Lord, that woman had a whole heap of secrets!

There was never a dull moment around that place. I quickly realized that the Peytons had their share of problems, jest like the rest of us.

Chapter Two

It was spring 1858 and I had just turned eighteen years old. This particular morning, Mistress came downstairs hootin' and hollerin 'bout why she got to answer to Massa every time she wanted to buy something fancy in town. She told him that he wasn't no real man if he couldn't give her what he promised before they got married.

Massa was as hen pecked as they come; and Mistress took advantage of him every chance she got. She treated that man like the dirt she walked on. To be perfectly honest with you, I liked it when she'd get to sassin' him in front of guests. He ain't have a clue how to handle that woman. He deserved every bit of suffering he got too. I ain't feel a bit of sympathy for that man either, especially after what he done to my family.

Mistress was a good woman and always greeted us servants every morning with a smile on her face. She'd even come and sit in the kitchen while us prepared meals. She'd talk from the time we start cookin' 'til us finished. She always seemed concerned 'bout how we was getting along there on Peyton farm; even asked 'bout our families back in the quarter. All of us felt real comfortable 'round the mistress, but we never, ever forgot our place.

I don't ever remember Miss Octavia changing her attitude toward us. She was one of a kind and kept us in stitches too.

Lord that woman had the strangest laugh I'd ever heard. It reminded me of a loud snorting hog. She'd get to laughing about something' that was funny to her; but once we heard that laugh; we'd start laughing too- 'cept we was laughing at her.

Mistress treated us fair, but Massa Peyton was the same old nasty heathen he'd always been. He'd stick his chest out barking orders our way. That man hated when mistress gave us good attention and always told her so. He'd tell her that slaves knew their place and she needed to learn hers. Of course she ain't pay him no mind, Miss Octavia did whatever Miss Octavia wanted...period.

Jesse Peyton always had something mean to say. He reminded us over and over that niggas was slow, ugly, ignorant and lazy. At first his words used to bother me, but then I thought,

"I may be so slow, ugly, ignorant and lazy, but at least I's smart enough to notice when somebody been spitting in my food and drink over the years."

After Mistress finished rantin' about how worthless Massa was that morning, she stormed right out that front door and had her coach boy carry her into town to buy that dress anyhow. By the time Massa Peyton could turn his head, Mistress was riding off the farm. He went chasing right after her too; as if he could say or do anything to stop her.

No sir – there was never a dull moment with the Peytons. It ain't take long before I realized that I was the only person left inside that house, not a soul in sight.

What I forgot to tell you was that in them years since my sister was sent away, I learned how to read.

That's right!

Remember Hope and Carter? Well, them chaps had what you call a 'tutor' – Mr. Littlejohn. That man used to come by every morning at 10 on the dot. Whenever he showed up, I showed up! I always found a chore close enough to where he was teaching just so I could hear them.

Hope loved learning; she used to pretend her dolls were her pupils and would get to teaching just like Mr. Littlejohn. Hope was a few years younger than me but that chile stuck to me like glue. We was always together and sometimes she'd walk down into the hollow with me while I was doing the days laundry. She'd bring her small writing board along with them dolls of hers and get to singin' the abc song, then afterwards she'd get to sounding the letters out – all 26 of them, one by one.

Even though I was busy with my chores, I always kept both ears open and one eye focused on that writing board so I knew which letter made what sound. Hope was a much better teacher than that tutor the Peytons was paying all that money to.

After a while, Mr. Littlejohn started getting suspicious of me hanging 'round so much. He told Mistress that he ain't feel right having nigras around while he was instructing the chillun'. I knew he told her that because I overheard it myself.

Miss Octavia never said a word 'bout it; she just made sure I done my chores away from the house while he was working. It ain't matter to me one bit 'cause by that time Mr. Littlejohn done already taught me all I needed to know to get by.

Now back to my story... Mistress Octavia and Massa went off and left me all by myself in that big house. I cleaned up 'round that house long enough to know where everything was; but it was Massa's desk I was most interested in.

The desk had a lock and key and he done all of his important work there. Instead of putting the key in a safe place, Massa Peyton would get lazy and just sit the key right on top of the bookcase in plain sight.

I walked on over to the bookcase and grabbed that key, all the while watching my hind parts. I opened up the desk and started sorting through several papers – most were too hard to decipher. I sifted through papers for about five minutes before coming across two pages that caught my eye. The first was a Deed with an "Inventory" and the other was a "Bill of Sale".

There that word was again "Sale" just like "Sell slaves". I started to sweat a little at that point, constantly watching my back, looking outside and praying to God that nobody walked up on me nosing around Massa's papers. The inventory had a few farm tools along with the goods sold from the property. At the bottom of the list were the names of people I knew from the quarter. I seen Cooper, James, Rodney, Lillian, Gustus; and then I saw Alice's name and nearly jumped out of my skin.

I quickly pulled myself together, 'cause I knew it was only a matter of time before somebody came strolling in through one of them doors. The inventory read:

"Alice sold April 13th, 1853 for $550"

But the paper ain't say where she went. I started to tremble nervously, mostly from excitement. I wasn't 'bout to

13

stop now after being this close to finding out where Massa sent Alice, so I kept right on snoopin'.

I picked up the deed and continued trying to sound them words out just like the tutor taught Hope and Carter to do. I read and re-read some more, attempting to form words that I could make sense out of. Then, as if God finally answered my prayers, at the bottom of the page were notes written about them folk listed on the inventory.

There it was:

"Alice, daughter of Rachel, sold on April 13th, 1853 to Royce Hutcheson, Lenah, Virginia."

I finally knew where that no count rascal sent my sister. I memorized the names of them other slaves and where they was sent, and then I neatly folded up the papers and carefully placed them back into the desk drawer. I quickly locked up the drawer and sat the key back on top of the bookcase.

Looking back, I know God meant for me to find them papers the way I done.

The Peytons ain't return home til about 7pm that night. They walked through them doors all hugged up on each other too. I knew Miss Octavia would get her way in the end. We prepared them roasted chicken with sweet potatoes. I got real nervous when Massa went toward his desk drawer and opened it up. He put more papers inside of it; thank God he ain't notice anything out of place.

I could hardly believe what I seen that day – all I could think 'bout was settling mama's mind at ease about Alice.

After Mistress finished her meal, I asked her if I could go and check in on Mama and Grandma. She ain't hesitate to let me go so long as I cleaned up first. I had to be back to the servant's quarter no later than midnight, which gave me two good hours of visiting time.

After we finished cleaning up, I ran as fast as I could to Mama's shack. She opened the door and hugged me like she ain't seen me in years. I'll admit, it seemed like weeks since I last saw her and grandma. Now I know what they meant when they said nigra girls was better off in them fields than in the big house.

House and field slaves hardly ever got a chance to mingle, 'cept in church on Sundays; and even then house slaves needed to tend to Massa's family, which took up most of the time you had to spend with your own family.

Mama and Grandma got three new slaves in their shack after I moved out. There was a young woman 'bout my age with her two colored chaps. Mama invited me in and us sat and talked 'bout how she and Grandma Josie been holding up. She told me that she worried about grandma working them fields the older she got and that Grandma Josie was the only reason she'd been able to make it on Peyton farm as long as she had.

I could tell mama wanted to talk to me in private so we excused ourselves and walked outdoors. Mama said that young gal in her shack had them two colored chillun' by Massa Peyton's nephew, Chris. She said the girl, Lettie, and Chris Peyton was in love with each other, and had their chillun' 'cause they was a family. Boy, Mama just laughed...she ain't never heard no foolishness 'bout no slave giving her body willingly to her Massa.

15

It was then that I sprung the news on Mama about what I found in Massa's desk drawer. Her eyes got real big, and then she yanked me by my arm,

"Gal! Is you done lost yo' damned mind?!"

She worried more 'bout my snoopin', than what I found.

Mama said that Alice was gone now and wasn't nothing more we could do about getting her back. She said life wasn't worth living if Massa took and sold me too. I felt like Mama had given up on Alice. I let her know that someway the Lord was going to get us away from Peyton Farm; and when that day come, wasn't nothing going to keep me from finding her.

Mama ain't speak no more 'bout what I said that night for fear some of Massa's snitches would hear and go back telling him. I was alright with that; the less anybody knew about me, the better.

The next day, I went about my chores like usual. I always liked working by myself; Grandma said, folk stay out of trouble that way.
There was a few house servants that I spoke to from time to time. Their names was Missy, Sam and Joby; they was all my Mama's age and grew up with her on the Peyton's farm back in Brentsville.

We was close, but not close enough for me to go spilling my business, especially 'bout me learning how to read. I ain't even tell Mama about that. Every nigra knew the punishment for reading and writing. I wasn't 'bout to risk my neck or my position in the big house by boastin' either.

One day Mistress called for me to get up to the big house, I was scared to death wondering if somebody seen me going through Massa's papers.

I declare that felt like the longest walk I'd ever taken. I recounted the events of that day in my mind over again. Who seen me and what excuse was I goin' to give? My nerves was rattling something terrible!

As soon as I entered the parlor room, Miss Octavia asked me to sit beside her and then offered me a cup of tea. Lord, there was no way my nerves would've allowed me to hold a tea cup steady enough at that moment.

Miss Octavia began to ask me what if anything I knew about delivering babies. I reckon I was in shock, but then I gathered myself together and told her truthfully that I knew nothing about it and that I ain't never witness nobody birthin' chillun'.

She laughed out loud and then told me a story 'bout how I reminded her of a slave girl she grew up with back on the Peyton homeplace in Brentsville. She said the girl was bright and 'cept for her condition as a slave; she would have been a tribute to her race.

Miss Octavia began to explain that she believed I would be a perfect candidate to learn that trade; but she didn't explain to me why?

Then she began to whisper a little as she spoke to me. She said, that she knew all along that I could read, but ain't mind it one bit. She told me that she also knew that I went nosin' through their papers that day too.
Lord Jesus, if 'guilt' had a face, it would be mine!

I was speechless and too ashamed or scared to death to open my mouth. My first reaction was to fall on my knees and beg her for mercy, but then Miss Octavia started in again with that loud, annoying laugh of hers, then added,

"Why do you think I lured Jesse away from the house in the first place?"

She just came right out with it. I tell you, that woman was something else!
She told me that she knew what Massa Peyton had been doing to Mama and it made her sick to her stomach and when she confronted him with it; he denied everything, but she knew he was lying.
Mistress believed that was why he went behind her back and sold my sister. She also told me that she would finally do right by Mama and Grandma.

Finally-*What did she mean by that?*

When she was finished talking, she told me not to run too far off; that she'd be calling on me again before the day was out. I went back to my chores happy as a pig in slop.

Other servants wondered why I was so giddy. It took everything inside me to hold on to the truth. One thing I learned early on was never to speak on anything that involved Massa or any member of his family. That's just asking for trouble and trouble was the last thing I needed.

Then I wondered whether or not I could handle being a midwife. I ain't know the first thing about bringing babies into the world; but I was anxious to learn if it made living on that farm a little easier for my family.

18

As promised, Miss Octavia sent for me to return to the big house, only this time she had company. A short, lanky but well dressed man that I'd never laid eyes on before. He stood there beside her and greeted me with a warm smile. That was the first time a white man ever showed me some manner of kindness.

He introduced himself as Mr. Davidson. He was Miss Octavia's lawyer and invited both Miss Octavia and me to have a seat in the chairs beside Massa's desk.

He sat behind Massa's desk and started signing several papers, and then he passed those same papers over to Mistress, who signed them as well. While all of this was happening, Mama and Grandma Josie walked through the door escorted by one of the field overseers. They looked as confused as I was 'bout being there.

My heart started pounding through my chest again, "Were we being sold right then and there?" All sorts of bad thoughts ran through my head. I blamed myself for being so stupid & careless, but most of all, for trusting a Jezebel like Miss Octavia to keep her word. I was numb with fear.

Mistress must've sensed the anguished look on my face.

"Mr. Davidson and I are signing a "Deed of Manumission," she told us.

Mama, Grandma and me ain't know what that was. Miss Octavia went on to explain that the document released us from her ownership; from that day forward we would be recognized a "Free negroes" with certain rights under the law. My sigh of relief was obvious. It took time for those words to sink in; even after we left the big house.

19

I still remember Mama's expression after mistress explained it all to us. Hmmm! There ain't words to describe it.

Mr. Davidson asked us to place our mark next to our names. Mama and Grandma ain't recognize their name, but I knew mine. Mistress showed them where their name was and gave them the pen where they placed an "X" in between the signature written by lawyer.

Then Mistress handed me the pen with a smile on her face. I knew how to read but I ain't know nothing 'bout writin'. That ain't stop me from grabbing hold to that pen and trying. To everyone's shock, I slowly wrote each letter the way it looked on the paper – when I was done, Mistress hugged me; so did Mama and Grandma. I'll never forget that day so long as I live.

Afterwards Mistress sent Mama and Grandma Josie back to the quarter to collect their belongings. I got real nervous 'bout us being out there on our own with no way of taking care of ourselves.

Mistress told me not to be afraid, she said us was going to live with a Quaker woman nearby, and that she was going to teach me how to midwife. She said that Mrs. Dyer was a God-fearing Christian and a widow living alone; she ain't have no chillun' neither.

Miss Octavia said the first time she laid eyes on me that she knew I was special and told me how she admired my spunk. She told me I'd need that 'spunky' attitude if I was going to make it as a free woman in society. I ain't know what she meant by that, but I reckon whatever she was trying to tell me~ wasn't all that good.

Mistress said that us ain't need to pay a thing, that Mrs. Dyer expected us to do the cookin', chores inside and outside the house and run errands for her. In return she'd provide room and board.

Miss Octavia said that Mrs. Dyer would tell us more once we got there. I remember getting up to walk out, when Mistress stopped me and asked,

"Ain't you interested in where Mrs. Dyer lives?"

I reckon I ain't think much 'bout it with everything else she done for us already.

She just laughed, "Millie dear, Susan Dyer lives in the town of Lenah."

Hmmm Hmm! Now that there was the cherry on top!

Chapter Three

I was the first one at the big house with my bags packed and ready to go. While I was waiting for Miss Octavia, Massa Peyton hurried through the front door.

That man looked at me like I had two heads, then asked what the hell I was doing standing in his foyer with my sack of dirty rags.

I looked him straight in the eyes and told him that I was a free woman and ain't have to answer to him ever again.
Lord, that man slapped me so hard, I saw star lights for the rest of that day.

That shut me up real quick. I couldn't do nothing but lower my head in submission. Next thing I remember was Miss Octavia running down the steps at full speed. She told that good-for-nothing coward to steer clear of me.

"Jesse you ain't got no right putting your hands on that child!"

Massa Peyton told her that I belonged to him and that she needed to mind her place. Miss Octavia laughed in his face and walked over to him,

"Wrong Jesse, Daddy left Aunt Josie & all her offspring to me as my own separate property; therefore I have the right to do with them whatever I please."

I can't tell you how surprised I was to learn that information. Miss Octavia told him that as of that afternoon, me, Mama and grandma had fulfilled our service to her family; and in return for that faithful service, us was granted our freedom.

That man's face turned redder than a maple leaf. The longer I stood there the more tense he got.
I knew I needed get as far away from there as I could before something awful happened.

Miss Octavia sent for her driver boy and waited patiently beside me til he arrived.
She even waited for me to board the wagon, and then gave the driver strict orders to collect Mama and Grandma and hurry up off that farm.

I worried about Miss Octavia after we pulled off, but everything in me knew that she would never allow Jesse Peyton to get the better of her.
Hell, that woman was more man than he could ever be.

As the wagon pulled into the quarter, I noticed mama there surrounded by all them folk she grew up with. She couldn't control her emotions; she wept openly, trying to understand why God allowed us to leave, while everybody else had to stay behind.

Them folk was all the family us ever known. Then I thought back to that inventory and told the families of each person listed which farm their loved ones were sent to; it wasn't hard to remember, since all of them was sent to farms in and around the Thoroughfare Gap.

I helped Mama and Grandma Josie into the wagon and we drove up off Peyton farm like us was 'High Class.'

As we made our way off the property, I couldn't help but think that it was the first time in my life that I'd ever been off that farm.

I never realized how big Peyton farm was until us rode through it. Nor the relief I felt once us made it to the main road. I remember the smell of sweet honeysuckle and wildflowers in the air and even though it was late in the afternoon, the sun's rays still beamed brightly through the mountainside.

In that moment I felt "free", I felt the warmth and protection that my God intended for us. I was overwhelmed with emotions.

Then my thoughts quickly turned to Alice and how she must have felt as she made the same journey years earlier. Mama pulled me close to her as if she could sense my thoughts.

We rode out of Haymarket non-stop until us reached the road overseer's on the Loudoun county line.

The overseers demanded to see our papers. I can't tell you how nervous we got when they pulled us over for the first time. I reckon every Negro feared being in the presence of white mens. The driver handed our papers over to them, along with a handwritten letter by Miss Octavia.

One of the overseers stared at Mama the entire time. Like I said, Mama was a beautiful colored woman which in her mind was more a curse than a blessing. They knew from Miss Octavia's letter that we was headed to the home of Susan Dyer. Both mens knew exactly where she lived and pointed the driver in the direction of Lenah.

Back in them days, once an enslaved person was freed, he had six months to leave Virginia, unless somebody spoke up for him. Miss Octavia and Miss Susan spoke for us – so us got to stay put.

We finally arrived at the Dyer residence about an hour
or so later. It wasn't as big and fancy as the Peyton house
but compared to the slave quarters, it was a palace.

Her fruit trees hadn't yet blossomed and the trellis's in
the front yard were overgrown with ivy and rose vines. We
had our work cut out for us around that place.

The driver pulled around to the front door and set our
bags down on the ground; after that he hopped back onto the
wagon and quickly high-tailed it back to Haymarket.

Mama was real nervous about meeting Miss Susan and
told me we should have kept on moving 'til us got away from
Virginia. I reminded Mama that I wasn't leaving Virginia
without Alice.

We picked up our bags and carried them 'round to the
back of the house, and then knocked at the door. A very
short, stout woman, 'bout grandma Josie's age, answered. It
was Miss Susan. She had been waiting up for us and was
glad to see us. She invited us right in and insisted us wash up
for supper.

I remember walking into my room for the first time.
There was a large window facing the back yard. I had a
three-quarter bed covered with stuffed dolls, two thick
patchwork quilts and two goose-feathered pillows.
There was an oak end table with an oil lamp and a matching
oak chest on the left side of the room. My floors were oak
and covered with a beautifully handcrafted rug.
That room was 'bout the same size as the shack I grew up in.
Hope's room ain't have nothing on this one. After I
freshened up I headed back downstairs.

Miss Susan hardly ever got visitors.
When we sat down for supper, she began to tell us about
herself.

Her husband Charles moved her north to Loudoun from Hanover County twenty years earlier. The Dyer's were Quakers and ain't believe in slavery. Her husband wanted them to move north to Pennsylvania 'cause there were more Quakers just like them up there.

Miss Susan told him they'd be more help to colored folk in Virginia than protesting up north in Pennsylvania. She was an Abolitionist, but asked that us keep hush about it. She told us there wasn't any sense in stirring up unwanted attention from the town's low-class whites; she referred to them as 'Crackas'.

After Mr. Charles passed away, she stopped attending Quaker services out at Goose Creek and joined the local Baptist congregation at Mt. Zion 'cause it was closer to home.

She said the bible is the same book no matter what church you're in; it's how folks choose to live by the book that mattered. She said all folks was hypocrites in some way or another whether they be Quaker or Baptist.

We learned a whole lot 'bout Miss Susan. She taught us how we was expected to carry ourselves as freed people in Lenah. She insisted that us learn to read and write. Miss Susan believed a person who couldn't read and write was enslaved in their mind; which is far worse than being a slave in them fields. "Every man got the right to learn and do better in life," she said.

She talked about how she'd lived up 'round folk that still enslaved in the mind and even though the 'good book' taught them right from wrong, they was still 'fraid of change. – So they kept repeating their same bad habits.

She said folk that talk about white superiority knew in their heart they was wrong, but they'd rather live with that lie 'cause it made them feel better about themselves, than the truth would.

Miss Susan was a real smart lady; she said the country had been split over the issue of slavery since the system was created over century earlier. She believed slavery was all about folk getting rich and went against the laws of God.

Mr. Charles Dyer passed away from pneumonia four years earlier and was buried on the grounds of the property. Miss Susan told us whenever it got too cold out for her, all she had to do was look right out her bedroom window and know her Charles was right there.

She was the best midwife in Lenah, and I would argue the best in all of Loudoun. She was called on for every birth in town; sometimes as far away as Lovettsville. But she was getting' too old to be travelling long distances; even too old to walk them back roads of Lenah all year around; which was the reason she wanted an apprentice.
She was only interested in training a Negro girl to midwife. She and Mrs. Beverly was long-time friends too; it was Mrs. Beverly who suggested me to Miss Octavia.

Mama and Grandma were real comfortable talking to Miss Susan, especially Grandma. They say the Lord put folk in your path that got the power to change your entire life. Miss Susan and Miss Octavia were folks like that.

Chapter Four

We lived in the Dyer house for nearly three years and just as promised, Miss Susan taught me all there was to know 'bout midwifing. She said that I was the youngest girl she'd ever known to birth chillun'. I delivered eight chillun' on my own by the age of 19; I surprised myself with how good I was.

Whenever we'd go to deliver babies, I had to follow two rules, the first rule was that I had to do exactly what Mrs. Dyer told me to do and the second rule was that I had to enter homes from the rear 'cause white folks ain't want no nigras walkin' up to their front door for their neighbors to see.
I never could understand how folks could be so honory; especially to somebody bringing their own chaps into this world.
I used to giggle inside 'cause I knew most of the time when they came callin' for us, that I's one of the most important people in that room during labor, but after that chile got out and the Mama was nice and healed up, them folk went right back to their old trifling ways again; least 'til the next one came along.

One day, I was called to help Miss Susan deliver a baby not far from our house. At first the woman didn't want Miss Susan to midwife on account of me. She and her husband hired a white nurse from the nearby town of Pleasant Valley.

Lenah's Veil

The child was breached and the midwife from Pleasant Valley had never delivered a breached baby before, so she sent for Miss Susan. Like I said, Miss Susan ain't midwife without me being by her side.

The errand boy told us that Miss Geraldine was bleeding real badly; so much so that he believed she had died already before he left the house.

When us got there Miss Susan went to the front door while I headed toward the back as usual.

This time was different. Miss Susan stopped me and told me that us was headin' through that front door together.

I reckon I'd gone 'round back one time too many in her eyes.

Besides, she was already offended that Miss Geraldine refused her help early on. So as far as she was concerned, Miss Geraldine needed us; not the other way around.

It was clear Miss Susan was going to do things her way that night.

I strutted my way to the front door right beside her.

A short, stocky man answered the door and right away noticed me standing next to Miss Susan. He looked at me, and then looked over at Miss Susan.

He yelled at me, "Gal, how dare you walk up to my front door —now Git up away from here!"

Miss Susan ain't say one word. She just turned around and started to walk off. Needless to say, he damned near broke his neck trying to stop her.

"Royce, I don't have the time or the patience for your foolishness. Your wife and child are going to die unless you check that pride of yours! This young lady right here is the best midwife you're going to find, black, white, yellow or green; I trained her myself!"

She told him that if he knew what was good for him, he'd better step aside and let me pass by.

To be honest with you, once I heard the name Royce, I would've been more than happy to shuffle my way right 'round to the back door. But he was desperate and allowed me to pass through the front door anyhow.
We rushed upstairs to Miss Geraldine. My skin was the last thing on that poor woman's mind. I could've been purple with red eyes for all she cared.
She was pale as a ghost and cold as ice; she laid there damn near lifeless, going in and out of consciousness from all the blood she'd lost.

Lord, I never saw that much blood before in my life. Miss Susan wasn't bothered a bit by it. She began to switch the baby's position in the wound. She explained each step she was taken and wanted me to pay close attention.

I must've been in shock 'cause all I really remember was grabbing hold of Miss Gerry's hand and praying as hard as I could for the Lord to save that woman.
Then a peaceful feeling came over me. I felt the Lord's presence right beside me; HE was the reason I was able to comfort Miss Geraldine through it all.

That woman bled something terrible; yes indeed, it was God that saved her that night, not us.
Miss Geraldine gave birth to a healthy boy. I stayed there with her for several hours until she finally came to.

Usually when us went to midwife, Miss Susan most times made me deliver the chile, and stay behind to sew and dress up the mother's wounds; while she checked over the baby and speak with the pap.
Sometimes we'd work all night long but us ain't never leave 'til we knew the Mama and chile was doing okay.

Most Mamas couldn't wait for me to leave the room after they gave birth, but Miss Geraldine insisted I stay with her. Mrs. Hutcheson thanked me over and over again for holding her hand and praying for her. She described the pain as being the worst she'd ever felt. I could tell she meant that too.

Mr. Hutcheson asked Miss Susan if I could stay a few weeks longer to help care for his wife while she regained her strength. He said he was afraid she wouldn't survive with all of the blood she'd lost already. He ain't want to risk her dying on him.

Miss Susan told him that if he wanted me to stay he'd need to hire me his 'self and that he'd have to pay me for my services seeing as though I was a free woman.
He ain't argue one bit neither. Can you imagine that?
I offered my services before he could get one word out.

The Lord sure worked things out for me. First he got my family freed, next he saw to it I became a midwife then I end out nursing for the very people who owned my sister Alice – with pay!

I took care of Miss Gerry day and night; getting her cleaned up, tending & dressing her wound, and giving her the tonics she needed to regain her strength.
Mostly us just talked about things to get her mind off of the pain she was feeling. Miss Gerry told me that I was a great listener.
I ain't have much choice, since she done most of the talking, I couldn't get a word in to save my life.

That afternoon as she slept, I gathered all of her clothes to take down for cleaning. An old Negro woman with a smoking pipe, sitting in her rocking chair pointed me in the direction of one of the laundresses. Walking through the

Hutcheson slave quarter brought back memories of my days on Peyton farm.

I was so caught up in my thoughts that I almost got lost. As I continued on I immediately noticed a young woman with her back toward me, scrubbing a pair of trousers. I knew she was the laundress on account of the baskets of clothes next to her. I yelled out that I had some of Miss Geraldine's laundry for her.

The woman paused, and then slowly turned to face me.

Our eyes locked, - it was like neither of us was sure we was seeing the other. It was my sister Alice.
She dropped the trousers in her hand and ran over to me and touched my face and looked me over.
It ain't take her long to realize that she was looking into the eyes of the little sister she was forced to leave behind many years earlier.

Neither one of us could speak; us just held onto one another and cried tears of joy. We barely got a chance to speak a word, when out of nowhere a Hutcheson overseer hurried himself over to us.

He looked down at me, "You must be new here."
Then he looked at Alice, "You get this gal straight, you hear?"

I was angrier that he interrupted us, than by the words he spoke.

"I am 'new' here," I answered.
I should've left it at that, but I didn't.

"If anybody needs to be straighten out, it's you." Then I told him that my duties on that plantation was none of his concern.

32

Lord, 'Freedom' can make you say the strangest things.

Boy~ that Overseer had fire in his eyes and his whip set to lash. He dragged me over to a nearby oak, preparin' to flog me.
All the while speaking the vilest words my young ears had ever heard. I thanked the good Lord Mr. Hutcheson came & stopped him in his tracks.
I signaled to Alice to run off; the last thing I wanted was for her to get caught up in my mess.

Mr. Royce yelled to his overseer, "Don't you touch that Gal!"

His overseer couldn't understand why Mr. Hutcheson stopped him. I reckon that he beat nigras for far less than what I said.

Mr. Hutcheson excused that low count cracka', then he pulled me to the side and asked that I stop showin' out in front of his slaves.
He ain't want to risk them uprising or getting too mighty on account of me challenging his overseer.

Mr. Hutcheson was the last person I wanted to offend; but I told him that Negroes were folks with feelings just like anybody else and that slaves ain't deserved being treated bad when they ain't done nothing wrong to begin with.

He paused a moment and threw his hands up in frustration. Mr. Royce was pleased with my work but he flat out refused to have any woman, especially a nigress, disrespect him in that way.

He said if I had a problem with how he ran his affairs, than I could see my way off his property.

I knew if I wanted to keep on seeing Alice than I'd best learn to control my tongue. I apologized for sassing him the way I done; even though we both knew I was right.

To be truthful, we both needed something from the other; otherwise I would never had made it off that property with my life.

I asked Mr. Royce if I could stay behind in the quarter a little longer while Miss Gerry was nappin'. He ain't mind so long as I wasn't causing trouble for him. I gave him my word I wouldn't, and ran off to find my sister.

When I caught up to her she darn near jumped out of her petticoat. She couldn't believe I was standing there after what happened earlier.

"Millie! Lord I thought that overseer was still by that oak beating the black off of you!"

We laughed, then I picked up one of her baskets & promised to fill her in on everything as I helped her finish up the days laundry.

I told my sister everything that happened to us after she left Peyton farm. Alice ain't believe it all at first, she thought I was lying like the devil. I told her that I ain't lie one bit.

She was overjoyed to learn that Mama, me and Grandma was still alive and well and living with Miss Susan right there in Lenah.

I promised Alice that us wouldn't leave Virginia 'til she got her freedom. She knew how much we missed her and loved her. As long as I had the breath in me, I was going to do everything I could to get her off that plantation, no matter what it took.

We laughed, and sang old cadences like we used to when we worked on Peyton farm. Then before too long, another

Overseer sent for me to get up to the big house. Miss Geraldine had awakened from her nap. I looked back at Alice and winked. She smiled and placed her right hand over her heart, the same way she done that day on Peyton farm.

I high-tailed it to the main house; when I entered the house, I noticed several visitors had stopped in to see Mr. Royce. I walked right on pass them and headed upstairs to Miss Gerry's room.
One of the men stopped me & ordered me to top off his drink. I turned to him, and then I turned to Mr. Royce.
I told that fool that I's the midwife for Miss Geraldine, but he ain't care one bit 'bout that none.

"A slave is a slave, ain't that right, Royce?!" he asked him. Mr. Royce paused like he ain't know what to say next. Then that old crow questioned him, "You ain't gonna make that darkie top up my drink?"

I could see by the look on Mr. Hutcheson's face that he was real uncomfortable.
I went ahead and grabbed the pitcher of iced tea, filled his cup, and then excused myself like a lady.
I only wish the pitcher was out of his sight; I surely would've spit in it!

Chapter Five

Mrs. Hutcheson healed up right nicely and even started to get around on her own. Their son was growing stronger each passing day. Mr. Royce used his milkmaids to suckle the chap. Them rich women hardly ever fed their own babies themselves. Instead they got their slaves to do it for them.

Mama told me that she and Grandma were used as milkmaids too. Grandma said them rich women ain't want to suckle their own chillun' 'cause they ain't want saggy breasts. That tickled me the first time I heard it.

Looking down at my own now, I can see why they didn't.

Miss Geraldine apologized for not calling on me and Miss Susan early on in her pregnancy. She said that she was raised all her life to believe that nigras could't be depended upon for important matters. I ain't get too mad at her for saying them things; in fact I appreciated her honesty.

I learned something that day. When the Lord choose you to receive his message, he gonna make it heard loud and clear; and he made sure Miss Geraldine was listening.

I found out the Hutcheson family lived in the county of Loudoun for generations, and just like the Peytons of Prince William, they too, married their kinfolk to keep the money in the family.

The Hutchesons raised livestock and owned over 200 acres of land in and around Lenah! They owned 56 slaves; twelve for the big house and the rest for the grounds. They had six chillun' already, but Mr. Royce wanted twelve all together. His wife told me that after that last chile, she was too afraid to have anymore. She had been with chile eight times and lost two boys. Her sons were buried at the Mt. Zion Baptist church.

Losing them chillun' hurt Miss Gerry real bad; I reckon her husband wasn't bothered much 'bout her feelings in the matter.

Miss Geraldine asked how my family got our freedom. I told her my story, yet all she could think to say was how difficult it must have been for Miss Octavia to part with such valuable property.

I paused a second, then I realized that this woman wasn't never going to understand me or those like me overnight. Sometimes if you have nothing good to say, it's best to hold your tongue.
Besides I had already been with the Hutchesons long enough and was ready to get back to my own family. I told her if she needed anything to send for me.

I packed my things and made my way through the backroads onward home. I couldn't wait to tell everybody how things turned out with Alice.

Usually when I walked through the front door, the first person I'd see is Miss Susan sitting in her arm chair knitting or quilting something or other; but not this time. I walked into the kitchen and there was Mama and Grandma preparing chicken's feet and rice. They were real glad to see me, but anxious to hear whether or not I got a glimpse of Alice. Miss Susan had already spilled the beans about me working in the Hutcheson house.

"You was a guest in da big house?!" Grandma laughed like the dickens. She was so tickled 'bout that. I couldn't get her to stop laughing.
I reckon that was a big deal to her; but to me it ain't matter one bit.

I nearly burst from excitement 'bout Alice and told them everything that happened from day one. Mama started to cry tears of joy and said she ain't never expect the Lord to bless her like he done them past few years.

Alice told me that there was a church not far from us, where colored folk, free and enslaved go to worship. Up to that point us was having prayer on Sundays with Miss Susan; after she returned home from Mt. Zion.

Mama and Grandma were excited to hear 'bout a colored church. Grandma Josie said she ain't feel right 'less she singing spirituals with our own people. She said us depended on each other in life, so us needed to pray together too. We agreed to attend services the upcoming Sunday.
The church was called Mt. Pleasant.

I'd been in the house for at least an hour before I realized Miss Susan was nowhere in sight. I asked Mama where she was?
Mama looked down sad-like and told me that Miss Susan came down with a fever the day after we delivered Miss Gerry's son. The fever had passed but she was still weak and unable to get out of bed on her own.

Mama told me that she refused to see the town doctor, Dr. Ryan. I ran upstairs and found Miss Susan lying in bed stitching a quilt. I walked over to her and knelt down by her bedside; not realizing that I was crying 'til I felt Miss Susan wipe back tears from my cheek.

She told me how proud she was of me for all I done since we arrived in Lenah and thankful the Lord bought her a new family to share her last days with.
"Nonsense," I said.
Truth be told, it was Miss Susan that was sent by God to help us! I told her how grateful I was for everything she done for us.

I mentioned the church over at Mt. Pleasant and how us planned on visiting; I promised to pray real hard for her during Sunday's service. She smiled at me then told me that her prayer's had already been answered.

Mama and Grandma came upstairs to feed Miss Susan. They sat beside her in that room talking and laughing – trying to keep her spirits up. I slipped out of the house to clear my head a while and decided to take a walk into town to buy a few things.

I had walked them narrow back roads many times before, never realizing Lenah's true beauty. The grass was always so lush & green; some of greenest grass I'd ever seen. It covered the hills far and wide; then there were the huge maples and oaks that shielded the suns rays above from every living thing below.

The sweet sounds of the hummingbirds and the cardinals. Old colonial style homes that sat upon the most beautiful grounds in the area; Lenah was a much prettier town to me, than Haymarket.

39

Lisa Noel

Folk made sure their slaves kept the grounds neat and well groomed; as if they were competing against one another.

As I continued on, an eerie feeling came over me. I began to wonder where was all the slaves?
I knew as fancy as those homes was, there had to be laborers and field hands nearby. It ain't take long to figure it all out.

Slave folk were rarely seen or heard. I reckon' to them slave owners, us Negroes represented their shame; and the only way they knew to deal with that shame was to pretend it didn't exist at all.

*Grandma used to tell us when folk tried to hide something or cover their shame, they was '**wearing their veil**', 'cause they weren't strong enough to deal with the truth. I reckon it's safe to say, the town of Lenah was wearing a veil of its own.*

When I finally made it to the Little River turnpike, I could see all the ladies in their fine dresses walking about shopping and catching up on the day's events. I felt invisible walking pass them folk; just like glass. Then as I approached the general store I saw a huge crowd gathering by the square. There was a man calling on southerners to give what they could to aide in the cause against the Yankees.

The more he spoke, the bigger the crowd got. He had them folk roused up with that speech he gave. He told them that the president was a 'trader' to decent white folk. According to him, Northerners ain't have no right telling them how to treat their slaves or live their lives and that it was "God's law" for niggers to serve the white man.

Lord my blood boiled with anger, but I knew that wasn't no place to be causing trouble. Besides, that fool looked like he could barely afford a pair of shoes, let alone a slave.

I walked into the General Store and accidentally bumped into a colored boy sweeping the floor. I'd been in that store many times over the years & never remembered seeing him. I asked him where the storekeeper was so I could give my list to him for to buy goods. He just smiled and pointed toward the back. He asked me to wait in front while he fetched the owner.

The storekeeper grabbed my list, collected the supplies and boxed them up for me. As I walked outside, I heard someone yell out my name. I turned and saw Alice running toward me. She had been out running errands for the Hutchesons and was on her way back home.

She wanted me to walk with her to the Hutchesons so we could talk some more.

Lord knows I wanted to, but I told my sister on account of Miss Susan's health that I could only walk with her part of the way; I needed to get back home.
Alice was sorry to hear about Miss Susan and told me she would say a prayer for her.
She also told me that things got better for them slave folk once I left; that Mr. & Mrs. Hutcheson weren't as demanding toward them as they once was. She still ain't let on that us was sisters to nobody neither.

As us approached Mountain Road, Alice asked me if I was still bringing Grandma and Mama with me to church on Sunday. I told her we wouldn't miss it for anything. Then she showed me how to get back to Miss Susan's house from where us was standing.

We had just hugged each other farewell, when a road overseer came up asking to see our papers. My sister quickly pulled hers out and handed them over to him. He made her high-tail it back to the Hutchesons, and then he asked for mine. I gave him my freedom

41

papers, and then he looked me up and down to see if I matched the description from the court register. He asked me where I lived; I told him I was a border in the home of Mrs. Susan Dyer.

He rolled his eyes and threw my papers down at me, and then he spit on me saying that I ain't have no

business walking around loose; as if I was a pet dog or something.

I gathered up my papers and ran home as fast as I could. I ain't stop to rest once 'til I made it through the front door.

Mama had been waiting up for me and wondered why I was out of breath as I walked through the door. I couldn't lie to her. Mama worried all the time 'bout them white folks hurting me.
She had some leftover chicken's feet and rice waiting on the table. I declare, them chicken's feet was good! I told her 'bout seeing Alice in town; Mama was so happy that she was finally going to see her big girl after all them years. Despite Jesse Peyton's attempts to break this family apart, the Lord saw us through.

Mama thanked me for having more faith than she had that we'd see Alice again and felt real bad for getting' on me the way she done after seeing Mr. Jesse's papers.
I understood that Mama was only worried about my safety.

While I sat there eating, Mama began recounting her days growing up on the Peyton farm in Brentsville. She revealed a secret that nearly made me fall out my chair. Old man Peyton was her real daddy which made Miss Octavia her half-blood sister. She and Miss Octavia played together every day as young'uns and was best friends once.

I mentioned the story Miss Octavia told me 'bout the colored friend she had. Mama smiled, then nodded in agreement; "That was me," Mama said.
She said the older they got, the further apart they became. Both of them had to learn their place. Mama as the slave and Miss Octavia as the mistress.

Miss Octavia used to be scared to death of Jesse Peyton 'til those babies started coming along. Hope and Carter softened that man up like butter; that's when Miss Octavia got all that sass in her.

She and Mama spoke about the day us left Peyton farm and how she apologized to Mama for taking so long to give her what the good Lord already promised her at birth, "Freedom."

I finally knew why Mama ain't mind it when Miss Octavia moved me into the 'house servant's quarters'. It all made sense; she knew Miss Octavia would make sure I was safe.
Ain't family secrets something?

Chapter Six

It seemed like me and Mama ain't sleep a wink; us was so nervous about finally seeing Alice. Grandma Josie got up with the roosters and had breakfast ready first thing. After breakfast us got dressed in our Sunday best for church.

We checked in on Miss Susan one last time before leaving the house. Mama welcomed Miss Susan to come along with us but she told us she'd rather stay home and rest some more 'cause she still felt weak from her illness. I reminded Miss Susan that I was going to pray real hard for her recovery.

We put some fresh apple cider next to her bed just in case she got thirsty, and then us took the horse and buggy and headed on up to the church. Us rode up a long, steep and winding road through that mountain and seen colored folk everywhere. Few owned their own houses, and even small farms. They had their own community safely tucked away; probably to hide from poor whites looking to start trouble.

They came on horseback; some on buggies, but most of them on foot. As us 'rounded the bend, we saw a log cabin. It was the church.
Back in them days the church sat on edge of a hill.

Lenah's Veil

We pulled alongside the dirt road and walked up the hill. Grandma Josie closed her eyes as the choir practiced inside; their voices as pure as heaven itself. We walked in and took our seat in the pews.

A colored man approached us dressed in a long black robe with a white collar around his neck; just like the white ministers who preached to us on Peyton farm.

Grandma and Mama whispered to one another, amazed at what they were witnessing; a colored preacher. He introduced his 'self as Reverend Cassius Bowman and politely stood there talking to us for a long time.
Mama asked him when the service was set to begin. He replied that they never started service until our enslaved brothers and sisters arrived. We thought most of them folk there was slaves, but they were all free just like us.

All those freedmen in one place; that really shocked us. Reverend Bowman told us the enslaved arrived every Sunday morning around nine o'clock. The landowners chose which overseers they wanted to stand watch while service was in progress; to make sure nobody ran off.

Mama asked him how he was able to convince all those owners to allow their slaves to worship there at Mt. Pleasant.
Rev. Bowman told us that he was the illegitimate grandson of one of Loudoun's most influential judges- Judge Bailey. The Judge's daughter, Elizabeth had relations with a laborer and died soon after giving birth to Rev. Bowman. Elizabeth was the judge's only chile. Judge Bailey looked past the reverend's skin color and done everything he could do for his grandson. Of course, the judge never recognized him as such in public.

Since Rev. Bowman's mother was white, he took on her freedom status, which was the law in them days. Rev. Bowman told mama that Judge Bailey convinced slave owners in the area that they'd get more work out of their slaves if they allowed them to pray with other Negroes. He believed that it was in the best interest of the slave owner to do this; and he was right. Slave runaways were rare in Aldie, thanks to Judge Bailey. Even though the overseers stood guard outside the church, he and members of the

congregation were still responsible for the actions of their enslaved church members.

Slave members took joy in being able to see mothers, fathers, siblings and children from neighboring farms that normally they'd have no access to otherwise.

"We have been blessed so far," he added.

Reverend Bowman was a single man, tall with light brown-skin, coal black hair and dreamy brown eyes. He definitely caught mama's attention right away. I could tell he found her interesting too.

Right about that time, the wagons came pulling up. Mama and Grandma hurried out with several others as they stood anxious to catch a glimpse of Alice. Then off the wagon she came.
Alice spotted us right away and ran over to us. Mama fell to her knees crying something terrible. Alice grabbed mama with one hand and reached up for Grandma Josie with the other hand; none of us willing to let go of her.

I stood there crying tears of joy that we were all finally together again. The church bell rang and everybody hurried inside to take their seats for the service. Mama kept a tight grasp of Alice's hand the entire time.

Lenah's Veil

Reverend Bowman preached up a fiery sermon that Sunday. Lord that man could preach the word. He said a change was coming real soon and us needed to be ready for it. That was the second time I recalled hearing about the war. He called it a war of Good vs. Evil and said it wasn't 'bout Northern values vs. Southern values neither; 'cause them northern folk was just as bad as some of the southerners down here. Then he said that the war was a testimony to the power of each side's faith in God and their

belief in the true principles of justice and liberty written in the Constitution of these United States.

Reverend Bowman was the first educated black man I'd ever met. I ain't heard no preacher before or since that could keep a whole congregation on their feet the entire service. I declare!
At the end of the service, Reverend Bowman asked anybody who was in need of prayer to come forward. I ain't hesitate at all, I went right on up to the altar beside him, determined to keep my promise to Miss Susan.

I introduced myself to the congregation and told them our story. I learned that not all white folk is hateful and I spoke to them 'bout Miss Susan and what she done for my family. I prayed for Miss Susan Dyer right there on the spot and then made my way back to the pews with my family.

Soon it was time to say goodbye to Alice and the other slaves. They were only allowed two hours of prayer, and then they needed to head on back to where they came from. I can't ever remember Mama and grandma so comfortable in my life. Reverend Bowman kept on talking to my Mama, and even Grandma made friends with a group of elder freedmen that day.

I walked off toward the back of the church. As I approached the rear, I came upon a cemetery with markers that littered the entire mountainside overlooking the valley below. It was the most beautiful, warm and peaceful graveyard I'd ever seen before. I remember standing there in awe of its beauty and wondering if this would be my final resting place.

A voice out of nowhere bought me back to the present.

"So yo' name Millie, is it?"

It was that same colored boy I'd seen in the general store. He told me he liked what I said 'bout Miss Susan and introduced his 'self as Nathan Whaley. He sho' was a handsome fellow, he had the same wavy hair that my Mama had and he smiled pretty too. I was so shy I could barely look at him.

Neither one of us knew the other was free 'til that day. I asked Nathan how come he and other free coloreds got two names, just like the white folk.

Nathan said that the second name is the last name of the pappy if you know it. He said if you ain't know it then you can use yo' Mamie's last name or any name you wanted for that matter. I asked him how come slaves only get one name. He said that his mamie told him that slaves not s'pose to marry each other; that they forced to breed like animals; and animals don't got no last names neither.

I couldn't help but frown at the comparison. He told me his mamie said all slaves want to be married but they know white folk won't allow it. He said if slaves started to marry one another - then white folk got to face the fact they enslaving regular folk, just like them.

"Shouldn't they know that already," I asked?

Nathan laughed and said that when folk got married their marriage and chillun' were considered blessed in the eyes of God his 'self. Me and Nathan got so caught up talking that I forgot all 'bout Mama and grandma at the church. He walked me back where Mama was waiting on me.

We shook hands and said good bye, then Mama, me and Grandma headed on back home.

All us talked 'bout on the way home was how much fun we had at church. Grandma and Mama said they couldn't wait 'til next Sunday, they said I did real good praying for

Miss Susan like I done. I told them I just pray the Lord was listening this time and get Miss Susan right. If anybody deserved healing, she did.

We finally got home and headed upstairs to check on Miss Susan. I'll never forget what us seen when we entered her room. Miss Susan had packed her clothes, fixed her 'self-up, put on her wedding gown and lay upon her bed as if she was going away somewhere.

In her right hand she held her bible and on her left hand she wore the engagement ring and wedding band that Mr. Charles gave her on their wedding day. She had a peaceful glow on her face with a slight smile as tho' she'd been waiting a long time for that day to come.

I couldn't help but shed tears after Miss Susan died. That woman taught me so much about life and how everybody deserved to be treated fair. We wanted to make sure she was sent off right proper so I made plans to see them folk over at Mt. Zion about arranging her funeral.

The following day I went to the Hutcheson house to ask Miss Gerry to accompany me there. I went around back of the house and knocked on the door and asked the servant if I could speak to Miss Gerry. She walked downstairs looking right fancy.

"My, My, Millie, how have you been?" she asked me. We sat down in her dining room to talk.
Word sure travels fast in Lenah; Miss Gerry heard all about Miss Susan's death and offered her family's condolences. I asked Miss Gerry if she could come with me to speak to the ministers at Mt. Zion to plan Miss Susan's funeral.

Miss Gerry agreed and was more than happy to speak with them; she didn't see a problem considering Miss Susan

was a longtime member. She suggested I let her handle the arrangements at Mt. Zion.

I asked how about her family and she told me a few days after I left their house that Mr. Royce was called off to fight with the confederate army against the northerners.
I wanted so bad to ask Miss Gerry why Mr. Hutcheson would choose to fight for such a dishonorable cause as slavery. But I could sense Miss Gerry was just as disgusted about that war for reasons of her own that had little to do with us Negroes.

Miss Gerry couldn't make sense out of south's reasons for the war. All she wanted was her husband back home safe and sound. She understood and believed all her life in the institution of slavery, but she also knew that this war would change the south for years to come.

Miss Gerry came a long way in her thinking from the first time us met. I was especially grateful since my sister was still considered her family's personal property.
I left Miss Gerry and hopped back into the buggy and rode for home. All I could think about was Miss Gerry, and whether she'd be alright raising all them chillun' by herself while Mr. Royce was away.

Then my mind turned to them slaves all over the south, who would finally get a taste of the freedom I enjoyed. I rode into town to pick up some things for Miss Susan's funeral reception, and passed a newspaper boy. I looked around and grabbed a paper telling him it was for my Massa. I needed to know how this war was going to affect my family.

When I pulled up in front of the house, I noticed a buggy and coachman standing nearby. I entered the house and

found Miss Octavia and Miss Beverly talking to Mama and Grandma. Miss Octavia was so happy to see me and I was just as glad to see her too. She came all the way from Haymarket to pay her respects.
We spent several hours enjoying their company until us heard a knock at the door. It was Miss Gerry and her brother-in-law, Tyus Hutcheson.

They came to prepare the body for burial. Lord almighty that woman worked fast. We introduced Miss Beverly and Miss Octavia to Mrs. Hutcheson. She told us the funeral was set for noon the following day at Mt. Zion and asked where Miss Susan wanted to be buried?

Mama and I agreed there was no other placed she wanted to be laid to rest, than beside her husband.
Tyus left to go grab some boys from town to help prepare the grave in time for the burial.

Miss Gerry also told us that the Reverend would preach the funeral service on the condition that Mama, grandma and me stood outside the church. He told Miss Gerry that the good and wholesome folk of Lenah ain't want any coloreds inside of their church.

We was disappointed but wasn't surprised none by it. We knew Miss Susan wouldn't want no evil man like that preaching over her body. She had always said us was her only family; so us had every right to be there to say goodbye. I thanked Miss Gerry but told her that we was going to find another minister to do the service.

Miss Gerry smiled, "Good for you Millie!" she told me. She asked us to let her know when the arrangements were made so she could attend and reminded us that Tyus would still get the grave and body prepared for burial. All us needed was a church and a minister.

Mama told everybody that the funeral would take place at Mt. Pleasant on Tuesday coming. "You ain't even ask Rev Bowman yet," I told her.

Mama said she knew that a good man like Rev. Bowman wouldn't think to deny Miss Susan a proper funeral. She said he'd be more than happy to do it. Hmmm. Mama seemed real sure about him preaching the service; I hoped so for our sakes. Besides I wasn't 'bout to argue with that woman.

hapter Seven

Mama convinced Reverend Bowman real easy to do the funeral at his church. He said Miss Susan's funeral would be the first time he preached a sermon to any white person in his church, dead or alive.

But he was more than up for it.

Tyus brought the body to Mt. Pleasant early Tuesday morning. I was a mess that day; I hadn't really slept a wink since Miss Susan passed away.

I never once believed that God didn't hear our prayer last Sunday, as a matter of fact, I think he did considering how peaceful Miss Susan looked on her deathbed. I can imagine her and Mr. Dyer finally back together again. The thought puts a smile on my face, even now.
Grandma Josie said that Miss Susan knew a long time ago that she was going up away from here.

Grandma said that living was a lot harder than dying. Living ain't scare folk cause us live every day, but us only die once. Grandma had a way with words.

We got ready for church early and headed up to Mt. Pleasant. I was surprised to see the number of white folks there to bid Miss Susan farewell; then I realized, she probably delivered or tended to most, if not all them folk that showed up.

It was strange really; most of the free blacks and well-to-do white families knew one another and was cordial. When I think back on it, it wasn't rich folk like Miss Octavia and Miss Gerry messing with us; it was them poor crackas putting us through all that hell in Lenah.

Several folks even came over to meet me being that I was Miss Susan's only apprentice. The service went on without a flaw. That was the first time I ever seen Negroes and whites sitting side by side. We sang spiritual hymns and thanked the Lord us had Miss Susan as long as we did.
Me and Mama talked 'bout it later and wondered, if folks could come together on this day, why not every day?

After the service was over, we invited everybody back to the house for the burial and reception.
Tyus Hutcheson buried Miss Susan beside her husband Charles. Grandma had spent the night before preparing a feast for mourners; everyone ate their full and all were thankful. Then before you knew it, they were all gone.

Mr. Bowman and Mama started to get real close as time passed. I was happy for Mama and Rev. Bowman; especially after everything she been through in her life.
After Miss Susan was buried, her lawyer stopped by and told us that she left me, Mama & Grandma all her earthly possessions, home, property, and furnishings. He told us that Miss Susan had extended family, but insisted us be cared for after her death.

Lenah's Veil

Folk in Lenah continued to call on me to deliver they chillun'; mostly out of respect for Miss Susan. I decided that if I was good enough to deliver white babies, there wasn't no reason why I couldn't help my own people.

I remembered what Rev. Bowman said about convincing slave owners to send slaves to his church and decided to seek out well-to-do white folk and convince them that I could deliver healthy slave chillun' for little in cost. I learned quickly that the only color that mattered to the rich was the color green; the less money they had to pay out, the happier they got, and the more willing they were to deal.

It made me sick to my stomach having to talk 'bout my people like they was less than cattle, but I knew it was the only way I could make a difference in their lives. I looked forward to helping slave Mamas and I was sho' thankful to treat them with the same care that I was giving to their Mistresses.

There were a few Mamas that I visited often. They'd give birth, and then nine months later they ready to deliver another one. I saw that a lot with the slaves. What bothered me most was whenever I'd return to see them; they never had the chile I delivered nine months earlier. I always wondered why these womens kept having babies back to back like that. What on earth happened to them babies?

One night after returning home from a neighboring plantation, I walked in to find my grandma peeling potatoes. Grandma could see that I was deeply troubled about something; so she ask me 'bout it. I told Grandma what was on my mind and she looked down a moment, as if she knew something, but wasn't sure how to tell me. Then she slowly started to speak.

Grandma said that enslaved womens was sent to breeding houses, to make babies with slave males from other farms. Slaves wasn't s'posed to breed in the same plantation 'cause the owner ain't want them mating with family members. She seen many a babies come out deformed on account of that.

The Mamas give birth and then when the chile was old enough they was sold off to other slave owning families or given as an inheritance to relatives of the owner. Either way, they was ripped away from their Mamas. That same slave was forced to breed again soon after giving birth to the one before – and rarely with the same pappy.

Grandma said that when you a slave, your chillun' not your own; that's how things had always been. Then I looked to Grandma and asked her if that's how Alice and me come along?

Grandma just shook her head; she knew I would find out sooner or later, so she just came right out and told me the truth. She said that all us was made in breeding houses and told me that when she came of age, she was expected to breed more slaves for work on other farms. Grandma had thirteen chillun' and out of all of them, Mama was the only one left.

She said that she was numb after birthing all them babies and ain't feel no bond with none of them 'cause she knew it was only a matter of time before they was sold away too. Grandma told me to close my eyes and imagine walking into a room and facing a complete stranger for the first time. He don't care nothing 'bout you and you don't care nothing 'bout him, yet you is forced to give yourself to him.

All the while both Massas watching what you doing and threatening to use the lash or sell you if you don't goes 'bout doing your business. *Grandma said them mens watched them the whole time, like they enjoyed it.*

Grandma's voice started to tremor as she continued to recount the awful details. Then she said, now imagine having to do that over and over and over again.
We both sat silently at the table for a moment. I took hold of her hand then I asked her about her relationship with ole Massa Peyton.

She said that Massa Peyton brought her from the Smith farm in Prince William County and that she bore eleven of the thirteen on the Smith farm. The last two were born at Peyton's homeplace in Brentsville.

At long last my Grandma was ready to heal from her past. She told me that the she had Mama and her younger brother Gabe by Ole man Peyton. Gabe died from fever at the age five. Grandma said the mistress knew the truth but could say or do little about it.
She was surprised at how well ole' Massa Peyton treated Mama and her brother. They got to play with his white chillun', just as me and Alice was allowed to play with Hope & Carter; which was how Mama and Miss Octavia became so close.

I asked her if he loved Mama and Uncle Gabe.
Grandma giggled and said sarcastically, "He loved them 'bout as much as a slave master could."
When I asked about her feelings for him and whether she loved him? My grandma jerked her head back and turned to me with a serious but cold stare and said,

"Chile, Can a woman love her enemy? Can she love a man that holds his own blood in bondage?"

Grandma said she blamed him for her son's death, saying that both of her chillun' should have been freed at birth just like his white babies. Even after Gabe's death, ole Massa Peyton refused to free Mama.

"Instead he gives me and your Mama over to his daughter, Octavia; like us less than a dog." she told me.

She added, "I hope he burning in hell with Satan! - No Millie baby, I ain't ever felt nothin' for but hate for that man."

I was sad that grandma never knew what true love felt like. Her whole life she was nothin' but suffering.

Grandma told me she used to wonder what became of the chillun' she gave birth to on the Smith farm. She ain't never focus too long on them 'cause thinking about

them was too painful for her. In her mind, Mama was the only chile she really had because God allowed her to raise Mama from birth.

I couldn't help but notice how cold Grandma's words seemed. It was like Nathan said, slaves was like cattle – after living and being called animals for so long, slave folk just started believing they was.

Maybe if I had spent more time as a slave on Peyton farm, I would have felt the exact same way. I also wonder how many chillun' I would have given birth to by now or worse, had to give up?

I asked Grandma about Mama but she told me that I needed to get my answers from Mama, not her.
When Mama came downstairs I asked to speak with her 'bout me and grandma's earlier conversation. She told me to leave matters in the past, but I insisted that she tell me the truth or I would leave right then and there.
Mama looked at me about the same way Grandma had when I asked her the same question.

She told the same story that Grandma told 'bout slave womens, then she told me that she was 15 years old when Jesse Peyton took her to the breeding house for the first time. Mama said when she walked into the stall there was a man 'bout 21 years old waiting on her.

Mama said that he had scars all over his back and arms from being whipped. He knew it was her first time and tried to be gentle with her. When they finished, his Massa yanked him by his chains, and then Massa Peyton came for her and put her in the wagon.

Then Mama went on to tell me that a year after Alice was born, Massa Peyton took her back to that same place.

"This time I walked into a different stall and I remembered what Mama Josephine told me 'bout doing this over again with different mens. I got sick to my stomach Millie, then I heard the door open and close but when I turned around it was him...the same boy who gave me your sister Alice."

Mama said she was at ease with him and like any young lady with chile, thought about the stranger throughout her pregnancy with Alice. She said that this time they was left alone and had a chance to talk a little before and afterward. His name was James, and he worked on the Barrow farm near Thoroughfare. Mama said James was dark brown, medium build, and good-looking. She smiled a little as she remembered their encounter.

"That was the night us made you, Millie. James made me feel like a woman and I never forgot him. I told Mama Josie that I was in love with James and that I needed to be with him," she told me.

Mama said my daddy was the first and only man she been in love with and said that Rev. Bowman was just as gentle as James was. She had begged Jesse Peyton to allow her and my daddy to 'jump the broomstick', but he refused. She knew slave marriage wasn't recognized by the laws, but a good Massa allowed certain breeders to jump the broomstick. This showed that the couple would only breed with one another, that way slaves at least felt they could have a mate if nothing else.

Mama said that was the closest thing to marriage a slave could hope for. Then again, Jesse Peyton wasn't no 'Good Massa'. In fact he got so angry by her request that he refused to take her back to the breeding house. Instead he decided to bring different slave 'bucks' into Mama's shack;

which was why me and Alice seen all them different mens comin' around when us was young'uns.

I asked Mama if she had any chillun after me and Alice. Mama smiled and denied having anymore after me. She said she prayed that God would close her womb so she couldn't bear no other chillun' by anybody but James, and she never did.

Mama said that Mr. Peyton thought she was useless, 'til he figured out how to use it to his advantage. He laid with Mama every chance he got.

She talked a lot about my daddy for the rest of the night and I listened to every word. I couldn't help but wonder how things might have turned out if my Mama and Daddy were together like normal.

Chapter Eight

Things really changed when them yankee soldiers rolled into Fairfax & Loudoun counties. Mr. Royce died at the battle of Goose Creek in the summer of 1863. Miss Gerry was devastated at the loss and spent a lot of time with her family in Frederick County, Virginia, not far from Loudoun County.

Mr. Royce's brother Tyus, the undertaker, ran the farm while Miss Gerry and the chillun' was away. He still allowed me to stop in to visit some of the slaves in the Hutcheson slave quarter.

I'd walk into town covered from head to toe worrying what soldiers on both sides was gonna do to me. There were stories about them raping negro and white women alike. If you asked me – they was all animals. Them Yankees that entered Loudoun burned homes, destroyed crops, and storehouses – they destroyed damned near everything in their path. Them was scary times.

Then one night us heard a loud bang at the front door. Mama and Grandma said as long as them soldier's was running 'bout the area like packs of wild dogs, there wasn't no way anybody was getting through our front door alive.

Whoever it was, refused to leave and kept on knocking. I carefully peeked out the side window and saw Nathan Whaley looking like he'd just seen a ghost. I opened the door and invited him inside. Nathan asked if he could stay with us for the night. He told us that the Yankees took everything they could carry away from the General store and then burned the store to the ground when they finished.

Nathan's mother escaped north a few months back from the Lewis plantation. He ain't have no real family to turn to. Nathan was the son of the storeowner, Mr. Buddy Whaley. Mr. Whaley once worked as an overseer on the Lewis plantation, where he met Nathan's mother Patty, a mulatto servant working in the Lewis home. Mr. Lewis liked Mr. Whaley so much that he allowed Buddy to take Miss Patty whenever he wanted her. This was how Nathan came along.

When old man Lewis passed away, he left Mr. Whaley $500; Mr. Whaley used that money to buy the general store in town and then he purchased Nathan from Mrs. Lewis and eventually gave him his freedom. Nathan wasn't treated no better by Whaley; he referred to his freedom as 'Hush money'. He worked in the store and ran errands for him, and in return Mr. Buddy gave him a room in the store and two meals a day for his hard work.

Nathan said Mr. Buddy kept his secret far from his wife – if she ever found out about him, Mrs. Whaley would go tellin' the whole town about it...just to make herself look good.

Nathan said them Whaleys was nothing but poor crackas trying to fit in with high society in Loudoun. The Whaleys hated Free Negroes, especially the freedmen on the mountain. Nathan said that many of the free colored folk in Loudoun was related to rich families in the local area. Some inherited their land from them while other colored folk inherited land from their ancestors who fought in the first American war.

Low-class folk like the Whaleys used the only thing they had to show power over Negroes; their lily-white skin.

Poor whites like the Whaleys was scared that negroes was going to rise and do better than them, which was why they harassed colored folk like they done.

Mr. Buddy warned Nathan's mama that if she ever told one soul about Nathan, that he would make sure she lived every day of her life regretting it. I told Nathan that Mr. Buddy should have been in the store when it burned down, not him.

Both of us laughed about that.

Mama allowed Nathan to stay. We talked so much that evening; we found out a lot about each other and just how much we had in common. Nathan ended up staying longer than one night.

He even got a chance to meet my sister Alice. He could hardly believe I was a midwife at such a young age and asked me too many questions to count. I gave him as much detail as was proper.

I also told him about our lives in Haymarket and how we got our freedom. Nathan didn't believe me at first 'til Mama and Grandma backed it up for me.

Me and Nathan got real close. He said I have good conversation and keep him on his toes. He told me that he planned on leaving the general store once he found other work where he could earn enough to marry and raise a family of his own.

"Would you ever marry a man like me?" he asked.

I was too afraid to answer that question and changed the conversation.

Me and Nate, as I started to call him, used to walk all over town together holding hands and talking about a whole lotta nothing. Yeah, I started to get real strong feelings for him, then one night after supper us stayed up and played a game of chess.
Miss Susan taught me how to play and I taught Nate.

Miss Susan said that chess made a person think about different ways of doing the same thing, and she was right.

As we was sitting on the porch, Nate asked me how I felt about him. I told him that my feelings was real strong for him; he smiled and said he felt the same way about me too.

He stood up from his chair and pulled me up from mine. It was like us was reading each other's minds. We walked into the house and down the hall into the spare bedroom. I remember gently closing the door behind me so we ain't wake Mama and Grandma.

First us started kissing and touching, and then us started to get more serious. I can still see Nate as he was that night; it was the best night of my life and he was well worth the wait. We fell asleep in each other's arms.

The smell of fried country ham woke us right up. I had hoped to get up and sneak back into my room before Mama came down; but that ain't happen.

Lenah's Veil

When I walked down the hallway, Mama was right there in the front room waiting on me.

She looked at me and smiled. She ain't fret none since I waited longer than most girls my age to give myself to a man.

Nate joined us in the sitting room where we sat down for breakfast. Mama ain't let on to him that she knew what us done the night before. We barely took one bite, when a loud ruckus outdoors caught our attention. Mama jumped up and grabbed Miss Susan's rifle.

Nathan took the gun from Mama and led us away from the windows and door. He walked over to the window, and then he turned to me and smiled, then opened the front door.

It was Alice!

Mama & me ran over to her. At first us thought she escaped from the Hutcheson farm since she had been running and was out of breath.

Alice could barely speak at first. Mama sat her down at the table and poured her a cup of water.

Lord we was scared to death; if she had run off, we would need to move quickly to get her out of Virginia.

Alice finally caught her breath. I can remember her words, "We free now, all of us!"

Me, Mama and Nate thought she had lost her mind; but she kept repeating it.

The president had freed all the Negroes, and now us got the same rights as white folks.

Alice told us that Miss Gerry came home and read the words to us herself.

Some of the slaves took what little they had, while others walked right off the property; ain't so much as say one word to Miss Gerry.

Alice told me later when she really thought about it, she couldn't understand why she felt like any of them needed to say anything to Miss Gerry, after all the Hutchesons was holding them all against their will.

I thank the good Lord we lived in Lenah, or else Alice would've had one hell of walk back to Peyton farm in Haymarket.
The Lord answered our prayers; the whole family was free and all under the same roof.

When I think long and hard about those years in bondage, it hurts me to my heart. I imagine generations of my family born & sold into slavery; some alive today who have no memory of me, or I of them.

Not knowing who your kinfolk was or where they came from is the hardest thing to deal with. Many of these Negroes don't know who their Mama or Poppa was. Just like Grandma Josie's chillun'.
I wonder if they think of her.
Then I think about the number of orphans left behind, cause their families was separated from one another.

Grandma told me once that negroes formed whole families of folks who were abandoned or orphaned. These families are just as strong today, as they were during slave time yet ain't none of them blood kin.
Over the years the truth about their existence slowly fades away, until the only truth they know is what's in front of them. Not knowing who our family is, will come back to bite us someday, I'm sure 'bout that.

I reckon that's one of the many 'veils' us negroes used to protect ourselves; but you'll never hear no body admit to it, 'cause the truth is just too painful to swallow.

Grandma came down stairs and saw Alice standing in the house and knew something big was happening. Alice walked over to Grandma Josephine and told her what president Lincoln done for our people and she nearly fell down the steps.

Grandma said she never believed a day like this was possible. She was overcome with joy and decided we'd celebrate the day by opening up the house to feed all those folk who were hungry and in need of clothing.

Chapter Nine

Grandma Josie kept her promise and opened up the house to ex-slaves making their way out of Lenah in search of family.

Rev. Bowman was right when he said that the war was between good and evil. 'Good' will always defeat 'Evil' in the end, no matter how long it took.

Old folks used to say, "The more you suffer, the closer to God you get."

Maybe 'cause them same folk was always calling on the Lord for help when they was afflicted. As soon as things start going their way, they forget all about what he done for them when they was lowly.

Which was why I thought it was strange when rich folk in Lenah started turning away from God, instead of turning to him – especially after losing everything they owned during the war?

Then again, those high falluting types ain't have God on their minds in the first place, when they was making all that dirty money. I often wondered what folk like that learned in church?

Like Miss Susan said we was all reading from the same book; yet some of us lived completely different lives.

After the war, some negroes moved into the north and west territories; and there was some who ended out returning to the same farms they were once slaves on.

They'd work a piece of land and live on it as tenants. Then once the crop grew, the landowner found ways to bleed them dry, like vultures.

Many ain't know how to read or write to challenge them nasty old land owners. Little by little our people's hope for a brighter future began to fade, along with the rights promised to us as Americans.

Every Sunday Rev. Bowman would preach to us about empowering ourselves so we ain't have to look to others to do it for us. Some of them folks was so used to being slaves; they ain't really understood what true freedom meant. They were still enslaved in the mind, just like Miss Susan said. I knew right then we had a long way to go to achieve true freedom.

Rev. Bowman had become a powerful minister in Aldie, a little too powerful for some folks in town. He and Mama really grew closer with each day, but even he knew he was a marked man. Being around Mama would only put her in harm's way if they was seen together.

He was right; a few months after his Empowerment sermon, Rev. Bowman was found hung by the neck and burned. The townsfolk called it a 'lynchin'', and a lot more of our mens, womens and yes, chillun' would be lynched in the years that followed.

I reckon that was their way of trying to get us to leave Loudoun, but us continued to stand our ground. Like Reverend Bowman said, good always defeats evil in the end – and someday those folk that killed Rev. Bowman was going to have to answer for their deeds.

Mama took his death real hard. I swear sometimes I think Mama made herself believe Cassius Bowman was my daddy, James.

Me and Alice stayed up with Mama every night and listened to her talk about Cassius; at times she referred to him as James by mistake.

Alice hadn't heard the story about James the first time Mama mentioned him. I had to tell her everything I knew about him. Alice was was tickled to learn that we shared the same Pap. Not many chillun' of slaves can say that.

Mama finally fell asleep. I noticed that Alice got real quiet on me. I asked her what the problem was.
She begged me not to tell Mama, and quietly led me into the front room.
Alice admitted that she had been to a breeding house twice while with the Hutchesons.
I was stunned at first, and then my shock turned to rage. Tears of anger rolled down my face. Alice was only 15 years old when Royce Hutcheson mated her with a slave belonging to Doc Poland.

She struggled to tell her story. Unlike Mama, Alice lied with her buck one time an' never saw him again.
She added, "I wouldn't know him if I saw him today."
I couldn't believe what I was hearing.

"What d'you mean, you wouldn't know him?" I asked.

She told me she had her faced turned away from him, and her eyes closed; mostly from shame. When I asked if they spoke to one another, she responded, "He ain't say nothing to me and I ain't say nothing to him."

Alice later gave birth to a baby girl. She nursed her chile for one year; Mr. Royce allowed her to name the chile – She called her Pearlie.

Alice described Pearlie as having had pretty curls in her hair, just like Mama. She was a good baby; hardly ever cried and she smiled all the time.
Mr. Hutcheson sold her off when she became a year old. Alice said it took her a long time to get over losing her baby girl.
"It would have been easier if Pearlie had died; that way I'd know exactly where she was." She said.

She later heard rumor that Pearlie had been sold to a family in Fairfax; but ain't know which one.

Then Alice wiped back her tears and quickly changed the subject.
She'd recently met a young man in town named Robert Crossen.
We sat on my bed all night talking about Robert and Nate; us fantasized about marrying them two boys.

The next morning I prepared breakfast and made enough to feed a small army. Grandma always said, don't skimp when you cooking, make enough 'cause you never know who going to show up. I made a big pot of grits, ham, flapjacks, fried apples and scrambled eggs.

Grandma was right as usual – I swear folk always knew when good food was cooking.

Two families came to the door that morning on their way out of town. We fed them and shared prayer and some good conversation. Ain't nothing like helping somebody when they down and out.

Later Nate showed up with a few people from the church. Everybody ate 'cept Mama and Alice.

Grandma became an active member in our church. She volunteered for charities at several colored churches and schools throughout Loudoun & Fauquier counties. She met our new minister, Isaiah Newman while feeding the poor at a church in Fauquier County.

Rev. Newman had been a guest speaker at a colored church in Arcola. He was born in Upperville in Fauquier and although he was an ordained minister, he hadn't yet found a church he could call his own.

Grandma and others from the church was so impressed by him that they asked him right then and there to minister at our church.

Rev. Newman respected Rev. Bowman's work and agreed on the spot. He was ordained after emancipation and quickly moved the only relatives he had with him from Upperville; his grandparents.

He was a smart man, not as fiery a preacher as Rev. Bowman, nor was he as defiant; but he kept our attention on Sundays.

I continued to work as a midwife, but me and Nate left Lenah soon after we were married in 1867. We settled into a three-room house of our own in Conklin, close to Nate's job. I birthed our first born son, Nathaniel James, and started delivering babies in the areas of Watson, Pleasant Valley, and Arcola.

Nate changed his last name from Whaley to Summers – he said he met a man once with that name and liked it.

We were happy for a long time and made a good life for ourselves in Conklin. Two years later I became pregnant with our second chile, and was forced to stop working to focus on our growing family. Nate and I joined Prosperity

Baptist located less than two miles from the house.

Everything was looking up for us, then one morning as he headed out to the mill, he held me closed to him and gave me a long kiss. He told me he loved me and walked out the door. He never returned home.

How could a man vanish out of thin air? For a long time I had no idea whether he was dead or alive. I was devastated, what was I going to do?

I'd just given birth to our second son, Charles. All I could think about was how in the world was I going to raise up two boys by myself?

I packed up our things and moved back in with Mama and Grandma. Alice and her family lived there too. It was a little cramped, but us made do.

Grandma wasn't getting' 'round as good as she used to, but she made sure she was in church bright and early every Sunday morning.

Mama and Alice took care of the boys whenever I went to deliver babies. Many families I'd delivered chillun' for left Loudoun; some had lost everything after the war. Others chose to up and leave once Yankee soldiers and carpetbaggers began pouring into the area.

They'd come in and buy up farm lands that had once been owned by some of Loudoun's most prominent families. The only good thing that came from those yanks being here was they had no problem selling lands to Negroes.

Other than that, them Yankees was just as bad, if not worse than the southern trash us had to deal with before & after the war.

Northerners were the biggest hypocrites; they'd preach their abolition, freedom-for-all in one breath, and then refuse to lend money to Negroes to build their own businesses. Whenever we needed something for the church, they hardly ever sold us anything without conditions.

Day by day I tried to get my mind off my husband, but it was impossible. There was times I felt guilty, not knowing whether he was dead or alive, then other times where I felt nothing but anger and resentment. That man was my world, and I felt like a damned fool putting all my love into him like I done.

I promised myself that I would never again give up my heart so easily. As the times changed, my outlook on life changed as well.

Chapter Ten

It was the winter of 1872; Robert accepted a job as Railroad engineer for Mid-Atlantic Railway. He and Alice moved their family to Baltimore, Maryland. I was real happy for my sister, but I admit, it bothered me knowing she was going so far away from us.

After Grandma Josie passed away, Mama put all her soul into Mt. Pleasant, same as grandma used to. I decided to stay, mostly 'cause the school Grandma and the other church members built, was nearby.

I took a second job doing laundry for the Ellzeys, while the boys attended school. Mama loved having them around – she said she always wanted sons.

.

Duke and Harriet Ellzey were born and raised in Aldie. They was good friends to Royce and Geraldine Hutcheson and were one of the few families that held onto their property after the war. They had seven grown chillun' but three were still in the home, their daughters Clarissa and Norma and their son, Warren.

Miss Harriet used to talk my ear off every time I'd come anywhere near her. She'd always speak 'bout the good ole' days before the war, when nigras used to work and singing spirituals as they worked the grounds. She missed hearing those voices.

Lenah's Veil

I wasn't the same spirited woman I used to be, my boys depended on me; so I knew nothing good would come of me putting that heifer' in her place.

One morning as I made my way to the Ellzey home, a carriage rode up alongside me. Someone from inside asked me if I needed a ride?
It was Warren, the Ellzey's son. I smiled and accepted his offer – Lord knows it was freezing out that morning. I went to step up to sit next to the driver, but Warren stopped me and insisted I join him inside the coach.

I remember sitting opposite him and feeling real nervous. Warren knew I was married with chillun' but he also knew my husband wasn't around. You know how folks get to talking 'bout things that ain't none of their business.

My nerves settled the more us spoke to one another. Warren told me that he was a lawyer and came home after attending the college of William & Mary; he expected to

open his own law practice in the town of Leesburg. He was the apple of his Mama's eye, a true Mama's boy.
He told me that Miss Harriet often faked ailments just to keep him close to her.

We arrived at his parent's home and the driver opened the coach to let us out. He couldn't believe Warren allowed a Negress to share his coach; that wasn't proper.
When I stepped down off the coach I kept my head held high and never forgot what Miss Susan said about maintaining my dignity.

He led me to the front door but I reminded him that if I entered his folk's home through the front door, they'd surely get rid of me, and I didn't want to lose my job.

"I'll handle them," he told me. Lord, that man was a mess! When us walked through that door together his Mama nearly fainted. I greeted his Mama and thanked Warren for giving me a ride that morning. I excused myself and quickly went about my duties.

That wasn't the last time I'd see Warren. He made it a point to greet me every time we were in each other's company. We had long talks about my sons and their education. We discussed family, church, hobbies and things us shared in common. Warren never mentioned the womens in his life, which puzzled me at first.

He was tall with a thin-build and had dark features for a white man. Warren had long dark eyelashes with piercing brown eyes that sparkled in the moonlight. Let me tell you, the man was fine.

I just couldn't understand how a man that good-looking hadn't been snatched up yet.

Since he wouldn't bring up the special lady in his life, I'd decided to coax it out him. I told him that I heard some of the ladies in town whispering about him and how smitten by his good looks and his charms they were.

Warren was all they said he was and much more. He was friendly to everyone he met – it ain't matter where they come from or how much money they had. He also had a way of bringing life into a dull room and always knew how to take my mind off of my problems; especially Nate.

That night I went home and found Mama there reading to the boys. I was so proud of her for learning to read so late in her life and I always told her so.
Every night she Nathan and Charles cleaned, clothed and fed before I got home.

Then she'd also make sure I had a nice warm plate of food waiting on me when I came through the door. She worried about my well being from the time I walked out the door, 'til I returned home.

She hated me being out so late and begged me to stop working for the Ellzeys. Mama reminded me that we ain't need to work, that Miss Susan left us well off enough to pay our debts and still have enough to get by. She told me that working as a midwife would more than cover any additional expenses.

I knew Mama was right, my sons needed me and it wasn't right putting them on Mama when she could be doing other things with her free time. At the same time I looked forward to working, just so I could be around Warren. He made my days bearable and I felt much stronger and more confident about myself after being in his presence.

But Mama and the boys were more important to me than some ridiculous crush. I promised Mama that the following

day would be my last day working for the Ellzeys. We sent the boys upstairs for the night and sat down in the front room. I made a cup of tea for us and we sat and talked 'bout Grandma 'an Alice; also 'bout her life back on Peyton farm in Haymarket.

Her eyes lit up when I asked her if she wanted to return there to visit Miss Octavia. Mama got real close with her in the years that followed; especially after that scum husband of hers got wounded fighting against them Yankees down in North Carolina.

I reckon' if I had to give them yanks a medal, it would be for taking that rascal down like they done. Lord forgive me – but after all the evil that man done, he deserved his fate.

I was so caught up feeling sorry about myself after Nate left, that I forgot all about Mama's needs. Not having Grandma around no' more had been hard on her.
We finished our tea and decided to pack for a weekend visit to Haymarket.

The following morning I made my way out to the Ellzey's for the last time. I entered the home from the rear and began collecting the days laundry. I could hear Miss Harriet in the next room speaking to Warren and his sisters. She dismissed them and entered the room I was in.

She greeted me and added, "There's something I must speak to you about Millie, it's..."

I interrupted her in the middle of her speech, telling her right then and there that the day would be my last. I explained my need to be with my family and thanked her for giving me the job. I also asked her if it was alright to finish out the day.

A look of relief came upon her face... "Why certainly," she added.

I began to walk away, then stopped, turned to her and asked what it was she needed to speak to me about earlier.
She blew it off and assured me that it was nothing important.
I felt real bad having to leave, especially after getting to know Warren like I done. I barely made it back down the stairs before Warren stopped me; asking me why I was leaving.

He gently took me by the hand and walked me into the sitting room. His Mama told him 'bout me leaving. A warm sensation came over me – a sensation I hadn't felt since I'd been with Nate.
I explained to Warren that I needed to put my family first for a change. He suggested I give up being a midwife, so I could continue working in their home.

He was even willing to buy another house for us, just so I'd be close by – He said he'd do whatever it took to keep me from leaving.

According to him, his day ain't start off right 'less he seen me first; He had the right talk that's for sure – but I stood my ground. That man knew how to put a smile on my face but I knew Warren wanted more from our friendship than I could give him. If he only knew how much I wanted him in return.

Both of us knew how dangerous a relationship like ours would be – maybe that's what was holding us back. I admit us treaded on thin ice.

I apologized to Warren and ran off to finish my work. It was hard finishing out that day but with the good Lord's help, I done it. I found myself thinking 'bout that man the entire way home. I was more upset over not seeing Warren again than actually losing the work.
It's never easy giving up good friends like that.

I was feeling real low when I entered the house. Mama and the boys was enjoying each other's company. I kissed them all but excused myself for the evening; I ain't feel much like socializing. Mama came up shortly after and asked me about my last day.

Mama could get the devil to tell the truth, if she tried hard enough. I told her about Warren, and how close us became. Mama shook her head before I could finish my story.
She told me that Warren and I would never be together and that whatever feeling I was holding onto, it was best to be rid of them quick. There it was, short and sweet.

*My Mama ain't never fool around much with words –
she made her point known whether you wanted to hear it or
not. I knew in my head that every word she said was right,
but my heart was saying something different.*

*I got my mind off of Warren and the town of Lenah and
decided to focus on our trip home instead. I spent the rest of
the night with mama and the boys and laid my burdens upon
the Lord.*

*C*hapter   *Eleven*

*It was a brisk morning the day of our trip. I tried to
tell Mama that it was best we wait 'til late morning before us
took to the road. Mama said, "Us get warm when us get
there!" Hmmm!*

*That woman used to get my goose sometimes. I reckon
her ways were settling in, they say that happens to folk when
they start to getting' old timey. I just done what she said and
loaded up that wagon with our things.*

Nathan and Charles was real excited 'bout heading out of town and seeing Miss Octavia. The last time we'd seen her was at Grandma's funeral.

We got underway headed into Haymarket. On the way there, we rode past countless colored folks coming in and leaving out of Loudoun. Some of them had set up camp on farmland. We saw chillun' without elders to care for them, folk asking for directions to this plantation or that plantation.

After all them years since the war ended, folk was still trying to find loved-ones. Ain't no way I could imagine wandering this world without my family.

Me and Mama talked about folk being sold, just like Alice was. She said she remembered seeing a whole family split apart once, each one sold off to a different owner.

"Things happened like dat all dey time gal," Mama said. Grandma told her when folk was sold off like that during slave days; most as little chillun' that when them chillun' grew up, they never know who they was going to hook up

with. Folk could be marrying they own brother or sister and not even know it.

We talked about slavery the rest of the way to Haymarket. All our people wanted was their freedom - they wasn't no more free that day, than they was during slavery. Even the freedmen weren't truly free during those years; us lived in the shadows too. A Freedman probably had it worse since they had little protection from the poor whites.

We finally arrived in Haymarket and drove down the long, winding road to Peyton Farm. As us rounded the final turn into the drive, us saw Joby and Missy – the house servants I worked with when us lived on Peyton farm. They was jumping up and down excited to see us.

Joby helped Mama off the wagon and took our bags into the house. He called for Miss Octavia. It ain't take long for her to come down once she heard Mama was there.

When us walked inside, Miss Octavia talked to us about Carter and his new found love. She said Carter had done real well for his 'self as a doctor and Hope married Taylor Neale, the son of a local rice planter. She ain't live too far from Miss Octavia.

After brunch and a little rest, Miss Octavia asked if us wanted to go into the Plains to visit Hope? Me and Mama couldn't wait, but the boys wanted to run around the plantation some more. Joby took the boys on a long hayride 'til us returned.

Watching my sons run around that farm nearly brought tears to my eyes. At their ages, Alice and I could only dream of playing with one another the way they were that day. Mama and Miss Octavia yelled for me to board the carriage headed into the Thoroughfare Gap.

I couldn't believe that the little girl who was always attached to me by the hip had grown up and is now married with chillun' of her own.
Everyone in town recognized Miss Octavia's coach and waived as she passed by.

We pulled into a local general store to buy penny candy for Hope's chillun'. Miss Octavia spoiled her grandchillun' as bad as she spoiled her own.
I just prayed them chaps wasn't as rotten as their Mama used to be.

As we left the store ready to board our coach for the Neale place, a man walked up behind us and touched Mama's shoulder. She turned to face him but appeared to be at a loss for words.
I walked over to Mama who by then was visibly shaken at seeing the man.
I asked if she was alright, but her eyes lay fixated on him. He broke his eyes away from hers and then set them on me.

The longer he stared at me the more I sensed something familiar about this man. I thought to myself, could this really be?
Tears flowed down Mama's face and then she confirmed what I already knew.

"James!" she called out with arms opened. I stepped back, still in shock and allowed them time to catch up after so many years. I realized that I ain't know much else about my daddy other than what Mama told me.

James apologized for interrupting our visit and kindly asked Miss Octavia if she could bring us back to his house, pointing to a nearby cabin, so that us could catch up on old times. Miss Octavia sensed Mama's need to be with James

and told James that she'd be sure and stop by the way back, if that was okay with Mama.

Lord, My Mama's face said it all; she still loved that man! James escorted Mama to our carriage and helped her in. I reckon he knew the sooner she left the sooner she'd return to him. He winked at Mama as the carriage rode away from him.

It wasn't easy pretending to enjoy our visit with Hope after seeing my pap, but us managed to get through the

afternoon just fine. Hope was doing well for herself and she and her husband seemed happy.
Mr. Neale was pleasant but didn't stick around long after we arrived. I s'pose he wasn't used to being around colored folks as equals; especially having them as guest in his home. He wasn't a rude fellow-then again, we wasn't there to see him anyway.

Mama was hardly thinking about Hope's husband or even Hope for that matter. Her mind was somewhere else entirely. I knew Mama was anxious to see her James again and Miss Octavia knew it too and graciously ended the visit. Hope hated to see us leave but we assured her that us would return; next time with the boys.

We hopped back into the carriage and made our way back into the Thoroughfare Gap past Beverly's Mill. Miss Octavia asked Mama if she was sure she wanted to stay with James, considering she hadn't really known him outside the breeding house.
Mama told her that she knew that man's soul like her very own. I agreed with Miss Octavia and insisted that I stay behind with Mama and my newfound pap.

Miss Octavia said she'd return in the morning for us, and that Nate and Charles would be just fine with her on

Peyton farm.
Me and Mama looked at one another and made our way to daddy's front door. We ain't have to knock, he must've heard the horses as us rode up. He opened the door and invited us in.

As soon as he closed the door behind us, he pulled us both close to him and hugged us while crying tears of joy. I could tell right then, that my daddy had a soft heart and was a good man. He had supper ready and waiting on us; roast

guinea and green beans with potatoes Hmmm! It was real good too.

We sat together a long time talking about me and Alice. Then daddy told Mama about his life before they met that day in the breeding house.

His Massa was Joseph Barrows, and he owned a small walnut farm near Broad Run Creek. He told Mama the day they met he was feeling real low; but he knew when he seen her, that she was a special light sent to him.

Mama could barely contain her emotions that night. He went on to say that when old man Barrows took him there the second time, he knew she would be there again.
I could tell James was real uncomfortable talking about his past in front of me, but he felt he needed both of us to hear his entire story.
Mr. Barrows died soon after he & Mama were together the second time.
Barrow's son Michael was a member of a Southern Abolitionist movement, and gave my pap his freedom. It took him two years to settle a petition in Prince William that would allow him to stay in Virginia, but thanks to Michael Barrow, daddy was able to stay. He said he took odd jobs on local plantations hoping to find us. He was even hired by Jesse Peyton to restore a room in the western wing of the

house that had been destroyed during the first year of the war.
He told us that he had pretty much lost hope of ever seeing Mama again, until us met at the general store.

"I knew all along I had chillun' with you Rachel and I tried for so many years to find ya'll," he said. Then he broke down crying as if he couldn't believe we were finally there with him.

Daddy's plan was to find Mama, buy our freedom and live in that very house we were in. The first owner he remembered was Henry Roscoe. Roscoe had a fit when daddy refused to breed with the local slave girls; so he flogged my daddy something terrible. Those were the scars Mama told me about.

Roscoe realized my pap wasn't going to budge; so he decided to sell him to Mr. Barrows. Mr. Barrows had more success with daddy after threatening cut off his manhood if he ain't breed with them slaves.

Daddy burst into laughter saying,
"That's the one friend I refuse to do without!"
Needless to say, he ain't force the matter no further. He said that was when he first saw Mama.

Daddy never married nor carried on serious relations with any other woman after Mama. Ain't that something? He admitted like most breeders or 'bucks' that he was forced to sire other chillun' by different womens, but it was Mama that stole his heart.

Then Mama spoke about her experiences with the Peytons. She talked to him for hours and giggled like a young girl. That night was the first time in my life I felt part of a 'normal' family. After all the time them two spent apart, they had a lot to make up for.
That meant I would be in for one long night.

After supper, daddy gave me a quilt and a goose-feather pillow. I laid down on the floor next his pot-belly stove while he and Mama headed back to his room.

The next morning Mama had breakfast ready bright and early for me and daddy. He was surprised, telling us that the last time a woman prepared him a meal, was in the slave quarters on Barrow's plantation.

"Hopefully it won't be the last," Mama said.

86

Lenah's Veil

I noticed a glow on her face like she finally found her place. Fate led us there that weekend and I quickly realized in that moment that my Mama wouldn't be leaving Haymarket that day or any other; not for all the cotton in Alabama! I only wish Grandma had lived to witness that day.

Her and daddy embraced and gave one another sweet pecks on the cheek the rest of the morning; then out of nowhere, my daddy pulled out a simple gold band. He got down on one knee and proposed marriage to Mama.
After all them years apart – daddy refused to wait any longer to take his bride.

Miss Octavia arrived with the boys 'round 12 noon. He invited them all inside his house. I introduced daddy to his grandsons for the first time. They was thrown off by the buck-head hanging in the front room, but other than that they treated him like they'd known him all their lives. My daddy could draw you right in with his charms, just like Warren done for me.

Mama told Miss Octavia that she knew the Lord led us down to Haymarket for a reason but she ain't have no idea it was because of James. Mama believed real strong that God was making up for all the wrong done to her in life.

She and daddy got married the following Sunday at the Thoroughfare Baptist Church. Daddy took Mama to that breeding house where they first met, and although for most colored folk it was a painful reminder of their past; for my Mama and daddy it was the first place they found one another, and love.
They made a vow to visit that place once a year to always remind them of the true enduring power of their love.

Chapter Twelve

Me and the boys spent three weeks in Haymarket; it was time to make our way back home to Lenah. Mama and daddy insisted I leave Nathaniel and Charles with them 'til I found a border I could trust to look after them when I got called to deliver babies.

Lenah's Veil

I told Mama that I ain't need a border and assured her that there were many folk in town I could have look after them if I was ever called on. She and daddy ain't need to spend their golden years chasing after their grandchillun. She insisted I bring them to her and daddy if things got too hectic for me.

Me and the boys bid farewell to everybody at Peyton farm and rode on home to Lenah. I hated to leave Mama and Daddy behind but I knew as long as they had one another, they'd be just fine. The longer us rode the more my thoughts turned back to Warren.
I missed him so; his beautiful smile, warm touch, and his laughter. I imagined laying in his arms in a field of wildflowers, no one else around for miles. The more my imagination ran wild, the sadder I got. Mama was right, there wasn't no way he and I could be together, no way at all.

Before too long we were in Lenah. As us pulled up the driveway, I noticed several dried up flowers and small boxes lying on the porch. I hopped off the carriage and cleared them away from the front door.

I opened the door and found letters on the floor that had been pushed under the front door. I picked them up and placed them on the table, then I grabbed the flowers and

boxes from the porch and sat them down on the couch. The boys were so exhausted from their visit; they ain't pay attention to the flowers and boxes. They ran upstairs to their room and took a nap. I grabbed all the bags from the carriage and sat them inside the house.

I grabbed the flowers, boxes and letters and took them into my room. It ain't take long for me to figure out who sent them; it was Warren.

I closed the door behind me as I read each letter one by one.

I could feel my knees wobble from nervousness. I sat down on the bed and continued reading. Warren wanted me to know just how much he missed me and needed me in his life. He said he ain't care that I was colored, he wanted to have me; and even spoke of moving out of Virginia just so us could be together.

I pray nobody seen him come through, the last thing I needed was to have my name caught up in rumors of miscegenation.

I read all of his letters and reckon I was getting a little worked up myself. The last time I had been with any man was my husband. It sure felt good reading Warren's words and being wanted by him in that way.

I started asking myself, "Why on earth would Warren risk everything for a colored woman like me?"

Then I asked myself, "Why not me?"

"What made them high society womens any better than me?"

Folks 'round here make colored womens feel like they nothing but toads. The sad part was that black folks believed the same thing.

Well I was tired of looking down on myself just to make others feel better 'bout themselves.

A few of the chillun' living nearby must've noticed us was home, and came right over.

Once my sons saw their friends, they jumped from their beds and ran right off to play with them

Lenah's Veil

I closed the door behind them and went back into my room. I started to open each of the boxes he sent; each box contained something different from the other.
One box was full of chocolate candies– while another contained perfume, and so on. He sent five gifts in all and each gift came with a separate bouquet of flowers. I was so touched by what he done that I got right up, grabbed my shawl and rode into town hoping to catch a glimpse of him.

I pretended to window shop, when all the while I was on the prowl for Warren. He almost ran me down coming from the bookshop. When us came face to face we just stood there smiling at each other. We were interrupted by a friend of his.

Warren introduced me as a friend of the family. He told me how happy he was to see that I'd made it home safe from Haymarket. I could tell that his friend seemed uneasy with our relationship so I immediately excused myself and told him to give my best to his Mama.

Mama was right, messing 'round with Warren would cause more harm than good; but damn I wanted that man something terrible.
I headed back to my carriage and made my way on back home feeling like a complete fool.

No sooner than I pulled up, Warren was riding up alongside me on horseback.

I couldn't believe how bold that man was, and aggressive too. I liked that about him. I started getting real nervous and couldn't help but look around thinking somebody followed him there or was watching us at that moment.

91

Warren put my fears to rest when he said, "Millie, I'd never put you and your sons in harm's way, I promise."

I told him to put his horse in the stable and I invited him inside. It was still early and the boys hadn't returned home yet. When I closed the door, Warren pulled me into his arms and kissed me for several minutes. He started to undress me, telling me how beautiful I looked to him. He knew I wanted him just as bad, so he lifted me up and carried me into my room.

We made love the entire afternoon, until us heard the front door open and close. I told him it was only the boys, and that he didn't have to leave, if he ain't want to.
And he didn't.

I asked him to stay put while I got the boys fed and settled. As soon as they ate, both of them fell right off to sleep. By the time I returned to my room, Warren had also fallen asleep but when I closed the door behind me, he woke right up.
Lord me and that man had one hell of night but he knew he needed to leave before sunrise the following morning to avoid being seen.

Although us wanted one another, there was no way either of us could risk being caught. Warren had a lot more to lose than I did, but he ain't care one bit 'bout what folk in Lenah

would say 'bout us being together. He was more concerned 'bout them harming me and the boys. Warren was my truest and best friend; other than the boys he was the only real friend I had in Lenah and I wasn't ready to give him up just yet.

Lenah's Veil

To be honest with you, I enjoyed every moment I spent with him. We talked 'bout everything and not only that, us knew how to satisfy each other's needs in bed.

Don't get me wrong, I wasn't a bit naïve 'bout what us was doing. It ain't take long for either of us to realize that our relationship was never going to be accepted by white folk or black folk alike. So us continued on in private.

I held on to our secret as long as I could 'til the babies started coming around. Mama and Daddy were so worried about us that they suggested we move as far north as possible to avoid getting caught.

After I gave birth to our fourth chile, rumors began to spread in town about me committing adultery; and my chillun's light skin bought me more attention than I needed.

One afternoon I received a knock at the door.
It was Harriet Ellzey, Warren's Mama. She came alone and refused to leave my house until I came clean about the father of my babies. She knew them babies were Warren's and wanted me to admit it right then and there.

Lord, I nearly fainted from fear.

Miss Harriet reminded me of the conversation we had the day I quit working for her.
"I was trying to tell you then, but you didn't let me finish. I thought your leaving would be the end of the matter," she said.

"But now you have made matters worse," she added.

Then I seen that she was just as anxious & scared to speak to me as I was to speak to her.

She told me that she loved her husband Duke with all her heart, but he never pleasured her in bed the way she needed him to.

Mr. Ellzey spent much of his time away from home on business. After a while, Miss Harriet grew bored with him and invited a Negro hired hand into her bed.

"He owed us one year of labor. He and I spent much of that year satisfying each other's needs. My lover did things to me that Duke never could."

She sensed that I was becoming uncomfortable with her story. She laughed, "I'm pointing out the obvious Millie, I too was young, married and partook in forbidden fruit just as you have."
I held my breath as she continued.

She went on to confess that she found herself with chile by the man seven months into their affair.

"I was forced to release him early from his service I never saw him again. In some way, I was angry with him for impregnating me; after all, I enjoyed the personal attention he had given me.
Needless to say, I sought every remedy possible to correct my mistake; even sought out tonics to rid myself of this child growing in my womb. However my faith would never allow me to murder the life inside of me.
The only person I knew able to correct my error was my mother; who smacked the daylights out me once she learned that I had gotten myself in the way by a nigger."

"Despite that, my mother was a very influential woman and covered my secret & our family's shame by having me admitted to a private hospital in New Orleans under a false name. By the time Duke returned home, she was there to

break the news concerning his wife's fragile mental condition.
Of course he was not to speak a word of it as the reputation of both our families depended on it.
My husband never questioned my mother's story.
Mother looked after the affairs of him, the children and my household."

I couldn't believe what I was heard.

She went on to tell me that she had planned on leaving the baby there in New Orleans, but when he was born, he looked as white as the other children.

"I stayed several months longer just to be sure." She told me.
"Be sure of what?" I asked her.
She answered, "Be sure that he was able to live as a white child Millie."

Lord have mercy - She was talking about Warren!

She continued on with the story.

Her baby boy had come out white as snow and remained that way. She fell in love with him& refused to leave him behind; instead she made up another story that she wanted to adopt a baby born to a close friend she met while in the hospital.

"Mother refused, but I threatened that if she didn't draft of the necessary papers for me to bring my son home, than I would tell father."

Her Mama did as she asked, and had false adoption papers drafted up. She even convinced Mr. Ellzey that Warren might help Miss Harriet get through her mental problems easier.

Their other children were too young to know any better. So when Miss Harriet returned home with Warren, he was immediately accepted by everyone as family.

Miss Harriet took a deep breath, as if she was thankful her secret was finally out. She sat down on the couch beside me and asked me again if my babies were by Warren?

I broke down in tears and admitted the truth to her. She held my hand, stood up and headed for the front door.

She turned back to me and said, "If you are going to continue sleeping with my son, make sure you do it away from here."

I was so afraid for Warren, he deserved to know the truth; but I knew it wasn't my place to do it.

apter Thirteen

If Miss Harriet had suspected the truth about us, than who else knew?
Whenever one of my chillun' was born, somebody in Lenah would start to pryin' about Nate's whereabouts.

I'd lie, telling them that Nate was doing fine, and that I'd let him know they asked about him.

I admit, I was relieved to discover that Warren was a Negro just like me; unfortunately the state of Virginia ain't recognize him as colored. In the eyes of the law, he was a prominent, white attorney. I can't begin to imagine what would happen to him if anyone ever found out he was passing for white or found guilty of miscegenation.

My crimes were even wicked; I was guilty of miscegenation, and also adultery; seeing Nate and I was still husband and wife.

I gave all my chillun' Nate's last name hoping that would cast off suspicion.

I ain't have no choice but to break things off with Warren. Miss Harriet's secret made me finally realize the dangerous game Warren & I been playing all them years.

Warren later agreed, and eventually moved out of Lenah for the sake of our chillun'.

In the years that followed, he met & married Kate Humphries of Hamilton. I admit I hated the idea of him moving on with somebody else, but with time, I got over it.

He built a grand estate home in Middleburg, where he now practices law. He and Kate have one son, Warren, Jr.

After his Miss Harriet died, Warren returned to Lenah to settle the family's estate. She saw to it that Warren got everything; even over the eldest sons she had by Mr. Ellzey.

He inherited the family home but allowed his sisters to live there; neither one of 'em ever married.

Kate was classy; and was the envy of every woman in Lenah. She may have been attractive, but that woman ain't know 'good sense' if it bit her on the nose.

Those heifers in town couldn't wait to get her alone and reveal all the rumors of our affair and the chillun' I gave him.
She listened and never once questioned them.

One day she came up to me and asked if the rumors were true. She looked like a jackass coming at me like that. I ignored her and walked in the opposite direction. I reckon no answer to her meant there was some truth to what folks was saying after all.

She was obsessed with Warren; I ain't too sure love had much to do with it. She had a hard time dealing with the rumors and saw me and my chillun' as a threat. I can't imagine her questioning Warren like she questioned me.

Our chillun' dressed in fine clothing; nothing like the clothes you find here in this country. They never wanted for anything. I'm sure them womens in town told Kate about that too.

Kate knew there wasn't no way I could provide for all them chillun' by myself 'less I had access to a lot of money. Warren saw to it that their every need was met; and did all his banking in Washington, away from the pryin' eyes of the townsfolk.

Warren sent gifts and money often to them under an assumed name. Us would take the train out there once a month to collect money from the bank account he set up for us.

Warren even hired two colored teachers from Philadelphia. One taught at the primary school near the church and the other taught at the secondary school near Arcola. He done all that just so his chillun' received a proper education.

98

He told me once; there wasn't anything he wouldn't do for any of them, or me, for that matter.

A few weeks after our first encounter, I saw Kate standing in front of the general store. I walked right on past her as if she was invisible. She snapped something terrible – and pulled me by my arm into a backroom of the store.

The storekeeper followed behind us. The thought of Warren, giving his 'self to a colored woman was too much for that woman to handle.
I wondered if she'd carried on this way, if she knew Warren was a colored.

She asked me 'bout my 'fair-skinned chillun' and if they belonged to her Warren? It took all that I had in me to keep from spilling the beans, but I understood full well that telling her the truth would be a death sentence for Warren.

"Mr. Warren and me ain't never have no relations, not now, and not ever. That man is too kind and honorable to be mistrusted by his own wife." I told her.
Those words really set her off!
She hauled off and smacked me on the face, and to her surprise, I smacked her right back.

Kate knew I was lying, but ain't know how to get the truth out of me the way she really wanted to.

She was stunned after I hit her, then she turned to the storekeeper insisting he call for the sheriff; accusing me of striking her with no cause.
Lord, them white womens could lie like the dickens!

The storekeeper walked off and sent for Warren to collect his wife.

The storekeeper and many of the townsfolk knew my reputation; which is likely what kept me from the pen. –

In all the ruckus, I made my way out of the store and back home as quickly as possible. I didn't want to be around when Warren showed up there. I still had strong feelings for him; and I'm sure he felt the same for me.

There was nothing to gain by staying in Lenah; I made the decision to pack my family up and leave as soon as possible. I done too much dirt there and I feared that Kate would hound us 'til the truth eventually surfaced.

I went home and had a long talk with my chillun', Nate, Charles, Walter, Josephine, Pearl, Frances, and Gene and I told them that us would be leaving Lenah for a while, but that someday I'd hope to come back.
They were sad, none more than Nate. He was 17 years old and wasn't ready to leave everyone he'd ever known.
Nathaniel was a grown man, and had a thing for one of the gals in church.

Mrs. Goins, one of our church trustees, welcomed Nate into her home just outside Lenah, 'til he could get a job and establish his 'self. It was real hard leaving my son behind; but it was a lot harder on Charles. He and Nate loved their younger siblings, but they knew they shared the same blood; like me and Alice done. Both of them held hope for years that their father would come home and rejoin our family, but

those hopes were destroyed when Warren and I started having chillun'.

I knew it was just a matter of time before Kate started plotting against us. I wrote a letter to Mama and told her that we was moving to Maryland to live with Alice for a while and that Mr. Powell Johnson, the church grounds keeper, rented the house until I could make it back.

Baltimore was another world entirely. Nothing at all like the farms Alice and me grew up on in Virginia. There were factories and jobs everywhere up north and our people thrived, making names for they 'selves. My chillun' were doing well for a long time 'til them "immigrants" started entering their schools.

Gene told me that them folk came into America from all over Europe– and they just as bigoted as the poor white trash down south. He used to tell me that them foreigners was welcomed here and given every opportunity to make something of they 'selves. Yet when us negroes who been here for generations ask for basic rights, they refuse to grant them. Gene was a real smart young man; like his daddy. I knew he was going far in life.

My son was right, I think of Negroes in the south forced to live separate and excluded from society, while MORE whites enter America and prosper over us.

Me and Alice enjoyed our time together, but I missed home. Yes, Virginia was home despite all its imperfections. There was opportunities up north, but I missed the small things that Lenah had to offer; family, friends, church, socials and most of all, fresh, crisp clean air, the smell of sweet wildflowers, fruit trees everywhere you turn, rolling mountains and lush green pastures. That's where I belonged.

My daughter's Josephine and Pearl stayed in Baltimore, near their aunt, and cousins. Josephine got married at 16 to Michael Hughes, and then Pearl took a job working as a cook in the McNair home, where she met her beau, Samuel Johnson. I ain't bragging none but my girls are the "Belles of Baltimore." They have them mens falling all over they 'selves.

101

My son's are perfect gentlemen, and just as handsome. They remind me that I am the only woman, they will ever love. But I know that won't last forever.
My Eugene found a work at a shipyard in Delaware and took up boarding with a friend. He wanted to be a lawyer, just like Warren – although I'm sure he wouldn't much appreciate the comparison. Gene planned on attending Howard University in Washington, D.C. the following year.

I told him he'd be closer to the University in Virginia than all the way in Delaware.
He said, "Mama ain't no jobs in Virginia going to pay me what I make up north."

I decided to tell them the truth about their father Warren and how us met. They had every right to know who their father was.
The fact that Warren provided for us meant nothing to Eugene. He told me that if Warren really loved them, he would've been there for them no matter what.
My son must've got his sharp tongue from Mama!

I reckon all my chillun' felt like that 'bout their daddy's, but I tried to teach them that ain't none of us here perfect. We do what us can and pray the Lord will help us the rest of the time. Maybe someday they'll understand it better.

In 1898, me, Frances, Walter and Charles returned home to Lenah. I can't explain just how good it felt

to be home again. It was difficult for them re-adjusting to small town life, but us settled in just fine. The first thing I done was pick some flowers from a nearby wildflower patch, and walked over to Miss Susan and Mr. Charles' grave. I prayed and found myself overwhelmed.

Lenah's Veil

I felt as if now my life was slowly coming full circle, that all veils were slowly revealing themselves to me.

I remember Grandma Josie telling me that Miss Susan had been waiting a long time to die. I now understand what she meant. In the years following her death I learned that Miss Susan didn't always defend Negroes against the system of slavery.

She and Mr. Charles were southern sympathizers. I found that out as I sifted though some of her old papers. According to what I read in letters, they ain't much appreciate blacks having rights equal to whites. When slavery was abolished up north, they refused to live amongst the newly freed Negroes. Instead they made their way into central Virginia.

Some of what she told me was true, Mr. Charles died from fever, but what she didn't tell us was that during his bouts of delusion he kept asking for the Lord's mercy. One of the lines in her diary claimed that he turned to her and told her that they was wrong; that the Negro MUST be freed to avoid God's wrath.
Miss Susan wrote that when he asked God's forgiveness, a peaceful calm fell upon him and he died right there on the spot.

She also wrote in her diary that the experience changed her life and that she would seek the Lord's mercy from that day forth. She said that once she asked the Lord to help her confront her bigotry that in that moment the Lord cleansed

her of all hate, greed, and selfishness.
She was seeking repentance from the Lord, and he used my family to set her on that course.

I knew from the beginning that God's hand was at work. Us coming to Lenah was no accident, just as it was his hand

103

that sent Mama back to Haymarket; and reunited her and daddy.

So, if what I believe is in-fact true, then certainly, it was God's plan that Warren and I met, fell in love and created this family.

Chapter Fourteen

It was April 1908, when I was awakened early in the morning by a loud knock at my front door. I peeked outside and was stunned to see that it was Hope Neale, all the way from Haymarket. I hurried to open the door and invited her in.

I could tell by the expression on her face that the news wasn't good. She took a seat at the table and told me that she didn't know how to tell me the news she had for me.

"Just come on out with it," I said.

She kept her head lowered as she told me 'bout my Mama having cancer and that it had spread to her kidneys. Hope told me that Mama ain't want to worry me and Alice 'cause she knew we'd get to fussing over her.

She needed both of us to come home right away.

Lenah's Veil

I took the news calmly and stood up from the table. I offered Hope a cup of tea and pound cake. She looked bewildered for a moment and then repeated herself.

I threw my hand up, before she could finish. I remember breathing real hard trying to catch my breath and found myself suddenly feeling faint. Hope quickly helped me onto the couch.

"I'm so sorry Millie...I'm sorry," she kept saying.

After I calmed down some, I got dressed and asked Hope if she'd drive me into town to get a telegram off to Alice and my chillun up in Baltimore.
When us returned to my house, I prepared a light lunch for us, and told her that as soon as Alice got there, that us would make our way to Mama and Daddy's house.

Hope stayed the night and made her way home the next morning.
Two days later Alice & my chillun' made it into town. We ain't waste no time; us boarded up the wagon and quickly rode into the Thoroughfare. Alice and me held hands like us done as chillun', both of us nervous and praying for Mama to hold on a while longer.

I couldn't help but think 'bout how Daddy was holding up and promised myself that I'd take care of him, if Mama passed on. We were both so upset with Mama for not telling us earlier. It makes me sick thinking of all that time us missed out on with her and daddy over the years.

Us arrived in front of the house; the mens unloaded the wagon while the womens headed inside. The door was unlocked so us made our way to the backrooms calling out to mama and daddy, then Pearl yelled,

"Mama they out back!"

There they was together, sitting out back on one of them rocking benches. Daddy was holding her close, with their heads resting upon one another. Me and Alice hurried over

to them and hugged and kissed them both. Mama lost a lot of weight. She told us she knew us would make it home to her. She and daddy just wanted to spend time with their daughter's and grandchillun'. Nathan even made the trip from Aldie, and us spent the entire day together, cooked out, and caught up on old times. We almost forgot all 'bout Mama's cancer.

Daddy told me and Alice that Mama would cry herself to sleep at night from all the pain she felt; he felt less than a man, 'cause wasn't anything he could do to ease her pain. Mama told Alice, sometimes she'd leave the house and go into the woods, agonizing from the pain, just so daddy ain't have to see her cry out loud.

The womens in my family was strong, I have to say Grandma Josie and Mama was the strongest womens I known.

We had a whole lot to talk 'bout, but Mama ain't believe in putting her burdens on her loved ones. She told me and Alice to talk to Miss Octavia, when the time come – and left it at that.

I told daddy that I wanted him to move with me in Lenah, but he refused. Daddy told me and Alice that he spent his whole life making a home for mama and his chillun', and if she died then, he was going to stay there in that home, 'til God saw fit to take him.

I remember there wasn't a dry eye in the house, when my daddy said that; and us knew he meant every word of it. After we cleaned up, everybody laid down for the night and slept peacefully. I couldn't sleep a wink, I was feeling real uneasy 'bout things and stepped outside on the porch.

Alice must have heard me get up 'cause the next thing I knew, she was right there beside me.

We sat there talking 'bout how bright them stars was shining that night. Then Alice turned to me and thanked me.

"What you thanking me for?" I asked her.

Alice said that Grandma told her a few months after she got free, that if it wasn't for me than us would never been together as a family. Grandma told her 'bout the vow I made to bring her home. Lord, I couldn't believe Grandma remembered that.

Alice said if I ain't find her when I done, it was a good chance that she would have never been blessed to spend the precious time she had with me, Mama & Grandma Josie; then she broke down in tears.

We both was grown womens with grandchillun' of our own, but still had no idea how us was s'pose to handle losing our Mama.

Maybe that's why God brought daddy back into our lives, so us ain't never had to feel like orphans. Me and Alice fell ended out sleeping on daddy's porch.

We made sure us got up in time to fix breakfast for everybody. Daddy walked from the backroom and went out in the backyard; he ain't say nothing, just started to pacing back and forth. I ran over to him, but it took him a while to stop his pacing.

When he did, the only words that came from his mouth was, "Ya'll is all I gots left of her now."

All three of us grabbed a hold of one another tightly; Alice broke down sobbing, but for some reason I wasn't able to squeeze no water from my eyes. Maybe it was 'cause I knew how much pain my Mama had to live with. I'd rather the Lord take her than for her to suffer one more day like she been. I was thankful the Lord kept her 'round long enough to spend one last day with her whole family.

Mama lived a full life, and in the end, she got her reward.

We buried Mama in the cemetery next to Thoroughfare Baptist Church. Daddy stayed in that house just like he said he would, and died a year and a half after her.

By that time Alice and me was used to losing folk we loved, but us also had families of our own and they was what got us through those touch times.

Life is funny. Me and my sister talked 'bout how us becoming more like Grandma and Mama the older we get. Like the old saying goes, "with age comes wisdom." Even the most-uneducated person learns some kind of lesson in life.

Alice and Robert grew tired of Baltimore and moved back home to Virginia. They moved into our parent's house and Robert became a deacon at Thoroughfare Baptist, just like my daddy.

Things were slowly getting back to normal.

One afternoon Frances and me decided to walk into town to buy sewing supplies for a dress I planned on making her. We walked into the store and there was Warren and Kate talking to one of the town folk.

The shopkeeper greeted me and started to making small talk 'bout me being the midwife who brought him into the world. Warren had never seen any of his chillun' as adults and was captivated by Frances. Like I said, our girls were beautiful young ladies. He couldn't contain his 'self and walked over to greet us.

Lord, if Kate had any doubt 'bout my past with Warren, that day surely erased them. Warren was gracious and kissed my cheek when he greeted me. Then he turned to

Frances and asked, "Now tell me, who this lovely young lady here is?"

Frances giggled and introduced herself to him. She knew he was her father, but she was careful not to show too much affection for him in front of folk.

We spoke briefly before buying our supplies and leaving out. Frances wanted to stay behind and talk to him longer, but I told her further she stayed from Kate Ellzey, the better off she'd was –thank God she listened.

I was fitting Frances for her dress when us heard someone knocking on the front door. I told Frances to stay put while I answered it. It was Nathan with a young lady friend he'd met in Middleburg. I ain't never think that boy was ever gonna settle down. He was a good man, but he couldn't be good to just one woman.

This time he showed up with a nice looking lady. I washed up and sliced a piece of cake for them, and then boiled some hot water for tea.

I yelled upstairs for Frances to come down. She was so happy to see her oldest brother and Nathan couldn't believe nobody came courting for her yet. I told him that Frances was the only one left in the house with me, so he'd better stop causing trouble.

We laughed 'bout it, then he introduced us to his fiancée "This here is my lady, Mildred." – He commented on us having the same name, I reckon' that was s'pose to get her points in my book. She was a nice lady, don't get me wrong and out of all the womens that my boys brung 'round me, Mildred was by far the sweetest of the bunch.

Mildred was a little older than him, which is just what he needed to settle him down. Us talked 'bout her family and where she came from. Mildred was told that she was born near Lenah, but was sent to live on the Lee plantation in Chantilly as a baby.

She ain't know too much else 'bout her family. She said the mistress of the house, Miss Esther Lee, took care of her all her life; even after the war was over.

She told us that Miss Esther liked the nickname that her last owner gave her. Nathan started laughing when they got to talking 'bout her name.

I asked them why they was laughing at her name.

Nathan told me, "It's nothing really Mama, just that Mildred got your name and Pearl's too, Ain't that funny?" "Mildred Pearl Lee."

I told Nathan that wasn't no nickname. Then Nathan said, "her nickname is Pearlie" get it Mildred Pearl–Lee? Then the two of them got to laughing all crazy like.

It took a while before I realized who this woman really was; and when I did, I nearly passed out.

Then Mildred told me that Miss Esther Lee found out that Mildred got her name from her birth mother.

Oh, Dear Jesus, it was really my niece, Pearlie! The girl I named my own daughter after. Pearlie, the chile that Alice was forced to give away. I asked her if she remembered anything else 'bout her Mama.

By that time Nathan could tell by the look on my face that something wasn't right.

Pearlie ain't have no memory of her Mama; she told us that Miss Esther, the only family she remembered, her and the negroes 'round the plantation she grew up with.

Them folks looked out for that chile just like Grandma said; slaves always took on chillun' that wasn't their own. Pearlie ain't miss out on not having a Mama, 'cause that chile was blessed with a plantation full of mamas to look after her. Lord, I's so grateful to hear that.

I got a sick feeling in my gut though. My niece and my oldest son had planned on getting married, and knowing Nathan like I did, them two was already having relations with each other. It was just like Grandma said, ex-slaves was going to end up marrying they own kin, and that's what was happening in our own family.

Frances took Pearlie out into town while I talked to Nathan in private. I had to come clean 'bout what I knew, but that boy ain't care one bit. He told me blood or no blood, ain't nobody keeping him from Mildred. He loved her too much to let her go.

I got tired of trying to convince him so I let it go. By that time Pearlie and Frances was walking back in the house with victuals from the general store. We cooked dinner and talked for hours, I knew I had to get word to Alice some kind of way so I invited Nate and Mildred to stay the week with us before they went off trying to get hitched. Mildred was happy to stay, but Nathan knew I was up to no good.

"Mama, I ain't keeping no secrets from Mildred, so us going to tell the truth, alright?" he told me.

I knew he was right, but I told him there in front of Mildred, that it wasn't my place to go running off 'bout something without talking to my sister first. Nathan realized quick that I meant business and he sat down and kept quiet. After supper, they turned in for the night, but I couldn't help but wonder how on earth I was going to tell Alice that the chile she gave away as a baby was alive and 'bout to marry her nephew?

Chapter Fourteen

I arrived at my sister's house early the following morning barely sleeping a wink and knowing how difficult this news would be for Alice to hear. I remember how hard it was for her to talk 'bout her daughter in the first place. Now after all these years, she was going to finally learn the truth about what happened to Pearlie.

Robert was surprised to see me and invited me on in. Alice was sitting in daddy's old chair reading the paper. She offered me some breakfast, but I told her that I wasn't hungry. She knew something was up, when I turned down her good cooking.

Robert kissed Alice and gave me a hug before heading off to the church. Alice was anxious to know what I was keeping from her. I told her 'bout Nathan coming home for the weekend and bringing a young lady with him. Alice was so happy for him and started rambling on and on 'bout young love. She stopped herself and laughed.

"Let me guess, you don't like the gal? Millie you better leave them boys and their wives alone or else you going to turn them away from you for good!" she warned me.

I ain't know how to tell her, so I just closed my eyes and came right out with it.

I told her that the young lady Nathan bought home was named Mildred Pearl Lee from Middleburg by way of the Hutcheson farm. My sister couldn't believe what I was told her. She quickly took a seat on daddy's chair and asked me to tell her everything I knew 'bout her – so I did. Then I hit her with the rest of it. My sister just covered her mouth in disbelief.

She told me, "You know I named her after you Millie, 'cause other than my baby, you was the only other person I felt that close to at the time."

I was so caught up with them two marrying that I ain't think one second 'bout Alice's reasons for naming Pearlie after me. Alice told me years before in my room 'bout Mr. Hutcheson allowing her to name her baby girl before she was taken away.

"Let's go!" she ordered. I ain't even get a chance to rest from my drive there. My sister wanted to see Mildred before Nathan got too hot-headed and decided to leave out before I got back. Alice told her daughter Lynn to look after Robert 'til she returned from Lenah.

On the way there, Alice opened up to me 'bout her past. She said that she always hated Lenah 'cause of all the painful memories for her there; 'specially those of Pearlie. As she talked I realized that my sister could've cared less 'bout them kids marrying one another. All she wanted was to make peace with her baby girl, no matter who she married.

When us walked into the house, Frances and Pearlie were preparing lunch. Nathan rushed over to hug his aunt Alice and pulled chairs up for the two of us. Alice caught a quick glimpse of Pearlie who was now in her late 30's.

"Come chile," she asked Pearlie. Pearlie walked over to her looking confused. She sat down next to Alice with a

puzzled look on her face. My sister told her 'bout the baby girl she gave birth to and how she was forced to give her precious angel away one year later. Pearlie knew she was looking right into her Mama's eyes and she broke down right there at the table. Nathan walked over to comfort her. Pearlie and Alice got up and walked into one of the backrooms to finish talking.

Nathan told me that he knew I was trying to break them apart, but he repeated his 'self, that nothing I done would matter, that he was going to love that woman 'til the day he died. Lord, sometime I wonder why my sons never listen to me.

Walter went and married one of them Thornton girls; he's doing real good but she got him all the way out in Washington, D.C. Then there's my Gene, the lawyer, he done found some crazy gal from West Virginia. Charles ain't do too bad; he married LuLu, a girl he knew since grade school – I reckon she ain't too bad, at least she minds me. Now Nathan- He go and find the sweetest woman he could to settle down with, one that I actually like; and she end out being his first cousin!
My luck ain't worth a sack of rocks.

It wouldn't have been so bad if us knew ahead of time, like the Peytons or the Hutchesons – at least their chillun' ain't messed up behind their family mixing. Maybe I'm making too much of it. Just then, Alice and Pearlie came from the room with smiles on their faces. I was so happy for my sister, but Alice still had to tell Robert and her chillun' the truth 'bout Pearlie.

I reckon like most slave mothers, after they chillun' was taken away, Alice must've thought it was better just to forget 'bout Pearlie altogether.

Lenah's Veil

Pearlie walked up to Nathan and told him that she loved him too much him to leave him be. She asked if he still wanted to marry her. Of course, he did and they were married a month later in Middleburg.

It wasn't so bad though, at least us had each other, that's what family is all 'bout. I just prayed that their chillun' come out normal.

In 1910, my baby girl Frances moved out, the last one. I took it real hard 'specially after she told me she'd be joining her older sisters in Baltimore. Her mind was set and ain't no need in trying to hold on after your chillun' tell you that. I's grateful that my sons lived nearby. At least I'd see one of them every other day.

To occupy my time, I started to midwife again, and then I found a young girl to train, just like Miss Susan trained me. She was a quick learner; but not quicker than I was at her age.

One night after delivering a baby in Arcola, I returned home and found a horse & buggy pulled up alongside my house. I always kept a pistol with me at all times; Walter insisted I carry one after Frances moved out. I hopped out and walked up to the front door. There sitting on my stoop was a face I hadn't seen in over 40 years. By God yes, it was Nate, my long lost husband.

Lord, that man was still as handsome as ever, gray hair, wrinkles and all, but that ain't stop me from smacking him clear across his face. I stood there and called him every name but a chile of God.

I opened my door and told him to leave my property; that fool told me he wasn't going nowhere 'til us had a chance to talk. He stood up and walked right in past me, like that was his house. He sat his 'self down on my front room couch.

I admit, I was relieved that he wasn't dead somewhere, but like I said earlier, anger overcame me when I wasn't worrying 'bout him.

I ain't even bothered to ask him why he left. Or where in the hell that fool been all these years. So I just stood in my kitchen close to my carving knives.

I ain't plan on using them 'less he gave me a good reason to. After minutes of silence I decided to hear him out.

I told myself, "If it took him this long to face me, then I reckon I'd best listen to what he got to say."

Nate asked 'bout his 'boys.'

"You mean to say mens don't you Nate, your sons are grown mens!" That's what I told his trifling behind.

His eyes watered up and he told me that he needed to face me like a real man and own up to what he done to us all them years ago. He told me that he lost his job the day before he left, but ain't have the guts to tell me. He spent his life too afraid of failing and in the end; he realized he could've made it through anything, as long as us had each other. Talk 'bout lesson's learned. It took him over 40 years to figure that one out!

After all my rambling, I started to remember the words I told my chillun'. That ain't none of us perfect. We do what we can and pray the Lord will help us the rest of the time.

Nate was only trying to make peace and enjoy some kind of happiness before he took his last breath, and ain't no faulting him for that. I forgave him that night and offered him a place to live, if he wanted. We was both alone and in some way, us still needed one other more than ever. I did it more for our sons and grandchillun' than for him; maybe I did it a little for myself too.

Lenah's Veil

Our family became closer after Nate came home. He accepted my chillun' by Warren as his own, and ain't mind one bit that they took his last name. The Lord saw fit to bring him home when he done, and I's thankful for it.

You know, this is the first time in many years that I can honestly say that I'm happy with my life. I thought I'd never get over Nate leaving me, or Warren moving on with Kate or worse losing Grandma Josie and my parents.

All my veils have been lifted and the truth was all that was left, no secrets, no pain - only peace. The end of my circle is in clear view of its beginning again, and my days are numbered. My road was a long and sometimes bumpy one – but one I'm glad the Lord allowed me to take.

Lisa Noel

Acknowledgements

*I dedicate this book to the memory of my father Stanley W. Smith, Jr. a.k.a "Fuzzy" and to his father, Staley, Sr. who helped introduce me to forebears through family history.
To the memory of my stepson, Francois, Jr. whose memory I will cherish forever.*

Special thanks to my husband, Francois Sr. for loving me & supporting me through every endeavor including my decision to be a writer.

To my lovely daughters, Ayana, Samira, & Chardonee, I love you all.

To my mother Juanita and my late aunt Linda Smith, for their love, encouragement, and faith in my ability to publish this story.

Last, let me acknowledge the inspiration for this piece, my family's matriarch, Mrs. Mildred Mason Smith. May her legacy continue to live on & prosper!

Lenah's Veil